# Deep Within

## the nectar of the Gods

## rests the Druze faith

Fadya Alameddine

First published by Busybird Publishing 2017

Copyright © 2017 Fadya Alameddine

ISBN 978-1-925692-23-5



This is a work of fiction. Any similarities between places and characters are a coincidence.

**Cover image**: Kev Howlett, Busybird Publishing
**Cover design:** Busybird Publishing
**Layout and typesetting**: Busybird Publishing
**Editor**: Beau Hillier

Busybird Publishing
2/118 Para Road
Montmorency, Victoria
Australia 3094
www.busybird.com.au

# Chapter One

Sarah Basheer prayed, as she did every night.

She dreamed of a cloudless blue sky, and glorious trees of flowering plum and cherry blossom, a magical puzzle-like scene of *tulips jonquils*. She imagined polyanthus of all colours and daffodils sprouting up in clumps through the velvety green lawns, some covered in tiny white daisies.

'The Lord's prayer is written in many tongues,' Sarah whispered. Her curious mind toyed with the existence of all things supernatural. She believed in aliens, mermaids, fairies, witches and wizards. She stargazed at the sky above and eagle-eyed unimaginable discoveries. Sarah trusted in divine spiritual entities watching, guiding and guarding her on her journey here on this blue water planet we call Earth.

Sarah felt a strong presence inside her soul that echoed she was here for a reason. She evoked a clear ingrained memory from the age of nine of a shining star through the kitchen window; it did not hover, nor did it frighten her. She felt it was observing her and Sarah stood motionless as it transcended to the skies. Growing up, she received illustrated bible books from a Jehovah's Witness door-knocker. There she paralleled the three wise men following the star, like the one she had seen.

Sarah detested her home life and everyone in it! With the exception of Mr Fitz, of course, her beloved high school teacher's name etched secretly in her heart.

***

It still felt like summer, with its crisp yet warm radiance. The warmth of the sun caressed Sarah Basheer's face, as she walked in through the gates of St Joseph's Secondary College in Melbourne in 1993, at the start of another school year.

She pulled her socks knee-high and adjusted her tie, which her traditionalist father Marrouf helped draw into a knot earlier. She was almost tripping over herself, having what felt like a two tonne bag on her back.

Sarah had attended this college since year seven, although never anticipated that her final year of high school would be etched in her memory, burning ever so vibrantly and lingering deep within her soul for many years to come.

The school bell sounded as teachers and students alike scurried through the hallways, barely noticing one another as they headed to their classrooms.

Sarah was introduced to her homeroom teacher, Ms Binder, a very short woman with beady blue eyes, her accompanying glasses with thick plastic rims giving balance to her face and strikingly long nose. Sarah was given the class roster for the year and discovered Ms Binder was her Legal Studies teacher. Sarah soon drew an impression from past students stating their dislike for Ms Binder, renowned for her razor-sharp wit and for singling out class pets.

Ms Binder read through the class list. 'Sarah Basheer?'

'Here, Miss!' Sarah raised her hand while sneaking a glance at the hunkiest guy in class, Chris Ricardo. His hazel eyes and tall masculine build made him a 'dream' guy who would melt the hearts of many girls. Sarah's heart thumped so hard at the very sight of him, that she fretted Chris may hear it!

In hindsight, when Sarah was in year eight she had asked one of her friends to ask Chris what he thought of her; his reply was, 'I don't even know her! Why doesn't she ask me herself?'

'Immature' and 'naïve' were Sarah's middle names; she'd never built the courage to face him, let alone say one single word to him. Chris was soon branded the most popular guy in the school. Word travelled quickly about Sarah's feelings towards him, and this sparked interest from the majority of girls who started seeing Chris in a new light.

Sarah felt she didn't stand a chance and soon realised Chris was now counting the notches on his prized belt, all thanks to her big mouth. Sarah learnt her lesson and never again expressed her feelings out loud or in the public student eye, 'the school paparazzi'.

Trying to stay focused, Sarah studied her timetable and noticed that her first lesson for the day was English. She breathed a sigh of relief; English and English Literature were her strengths.

Sarah hurled her books clumsily into the allocated locker. It was situated at about her height, which was five feet four inches, or 'fivish' as some would say.

Sarah didn't inherit her mother Jamal's height, fine hair or beauty; instead she was a short, pimply faced, frizzy-haired girl with a pinch of paranoia. Jamal would often say that 'one's imperfections make you beautiful and unique'. Sarah would dismiss this statement, bearing in mind that her one and only brother, Dan, would constantly call her 'Dot to Dot Face', 'Frizzos' and 'Short Arse' to name a few of his comments.

Sarah secured her locker and combination lock and took her English folder, diary and pencil case with her. She hastily proceeded to her English class, already forgetting the number sequence for her padlock. She had jotted the number down on a tiny piece of paper – that was now in amongst her scattered books. Sarah instantly imagined Dan smirking and calling her 'scatterbrain'.

Sarah entered classroom 109 for the very first time and gently wiped her brow with her sleeve. She was sweating now, thinking of how embarrassed she'd be when asking Ms Binder for a bolt cutter.

The classroom smelt familiar, like rich burning cedar or old schoolbooks, a musky pine incense of scented candles. Sarah, trying to remain inconspicuous, placed her books on the desk in the centre of the classroom. She observed a rather young teacher and gathered that he must be new to the school.

This teacher was confident in his approach when he directed the class and stood with great poise, saying, 'Good morning, class! My name is Mr Fitzpatrick, or you may call me Mr Fitz for short if you like.

'I'm sure you've all noticed that I am new to your school. As a matter of fact, this is my first year of teaching. I feel privileged to be teaching year twelve English and English Literature this year. Now enough about me. I want to get to know you all individually, so I will call your name and mark off the class list as I go. Also, could you please state what your intentions are after you graduate from high school?'

Mr Fitzpatrick pointed to a rather plump boy who was touted the class clown and had a slight stutter.

'My name is Br … Brad. Tan … ker.' Brad hesitated, and then resumed after the distant chuckle in the background. 'I know what you are all thinking … But … I will amount to some … thing one day – and when I grow up I want to be just like Thomas … The Tank Engine,' said Brad with a grin from ear to ear.

Before Brad could finish, there was an upheaval of laughter.

Mr Fitzpatrick nodded in disapproval. 'Sit down, Brad … being facetious will get you nowhere in my class. I can promise you that.'

Brad huffed and mumbled under his breath 'Jeepers … creepers, man's got no sense of humour.' Brad grudgingly sat down, raised his eyebrows at Sarah who was seated next to him and spurted, 'he's a gay lord.'

Sarah didn't look the slightest bit impressed. She couldn't help but notice, after studying Mr Fitz's face, how blue his eyes were and began to sing under her breath Elton John's song 'Blue Eyes'.

However, slipping back into reality, she thought he was really not her type, in comparison to the Chris Ricardos of the world. Mr Fitz wore a woollen coloured sweater, brown slacks and peanut grizzly Doc Martin shoes. He seemed of Irish heritage (without the accent) and had short, auburn, curly hair, an awkward body image and a short frame. Even the way he walked seemed strange, as if walking on the tips of his toes.

Sarah was instantly fascinated by him; she couldn't resist staring at Mr Fitz and hoped this would not be mistaken as attraction. She was a conscientious student who ranked quite highly in the class, so Mr Fitz would notice her academic work.

Eventually Mr Fitz's eyes fixated on Sarah's and for a second, no more, she felt her face redden. Mr Fitz motioned for Sarah to address the class.

'As you all know, my name is Sarah Basheer and I would like to get into criminal or civil law.' Sarah said this only to impress Mr Fitz, to portray herself as a smart girl who knew what direction she was heading in life, but in all truth she knew very well what her strict parents had in store for her. It wasn't university, but a ring on her finger before she turned nineteen.

Marrouf spoke often about Druze doctrines being kept secret, even from the majority of members.

'We are Muwahhidun,' he'd say, meaning monotheists (belief in only one God). 'Heavily influenced by Greek and Hindu philosophy, our religion is confined, with conversion either to or from the sect forbidden. Scriptures are drawn from the Bible, the Quran, and Sufi parables; our religious text is called *Kitab al-Hikma* (The "Book of Wisdom").' Sarah's parents believed in reincarnation, a key belief of their faith. They often stated that an ancient memory of a past life impacted on a future responsibility, placed deep within you before coming into this world. Sarah thought this to be true, suspecting she was rather an old soul and her kindred spirit was lurking in the world somewhere, anticipating her return. Sarah hadn't found him – or perhaps she had and didn't know it yet. She often questioned her religion and that scepticism grew during her adolescent years.

Sarah couldn't fathom why this so-called religious text, the 'Book of Wisdom', was not sold in all good bookstores or openly displayed to the general public. The Bible and Quran, on the other hand, are widely recognised and shared around the world. Why this cloak of secrecy which renders the Book of

Wisdom all the more mysterious to many Druze themselves? Sarah's questions came to no avail. Yet, one thing she knew for sure was her belief in some greater positive force, giving her strength day by day.

After all the students had completed their introductions, Mr Fitz instructed the class: 'I would like you all to jot down your strengths and weaknesses for this subject and when you have completed this task, put your work on my desk, thanks.'

Sarah knew instantly what her strengths were, although as much as she accepted her weaknesses (and indeed there were many), she couldn't pinpoint them at this time – or perhaps didn't want to. Sarah noted her strengths quickly and waited for others to hand in their work in order to slip her paper in amongst them. As she walked over to Mr Fitz's desk, he looked up at her and gently smiled. Sarah felt a little at ease now and flashed him her pearly whites, her beautiful smile lighting up her entire face.

She turned away slightly and Mr Fitz said, 'Sarah Basheer! Did I pronounce your family name correctly?'

'Yes, that's fine, Mr Fitz. *Basheer,* putting a little emphasis on the "e"s.'

'Okay, and do you mind me asking your nationality?' Mr Fitz said in an inquisitive tone.

'I … I'm Arabic. You know, Lebanese!'

The school bell played its monotonous hullabaloo – just like Sarah's old astrological alarm clock, only louder – and this time she was relieved to hear it. She was quite flustered and noticed her fellow classmates' curious stares and whispers. Even Brad chanted, 'Teacher's pet, teacher's pet, you can bet Sarah's the teacher's pet!' Sarah glared at Brad so hard that if he were a mirror, he would have shattered into zillions of tiny little pieces.

Sarah turned to Mr Fitz and sighed. 'Sorry sir, you'll have to excuse me.' She walked out of room 109, giving Brad a little nudge as he slowly walked passed her. She headed reluctantly to her dreaded locker, feeling stupid from forgetting to ask for a bolt cutter.

'Hey, Sarah!' Leila yelled eagerly, waving her hands in the air. Sarah turned slightly and tried to ignore the familiar voice. She was preoccupied and fiddled with her combination lock in an attempt to hear a faint clicking sound, but the only sound she could hear was an annoying chuckle from her friend.

Sarah bashed her locker with her bare fist. 'Damn it, damn this locker and damn you Leila!'

'Well Sarah, you're damned if you do and you're damned if you don't! What did I do? I just got here. What's wrong anyway?' Leila said, baffled.

'Don't ask. I don't know how this year is going to pan out, but it's started out badly with Ms Binder being my homeroom as well as Legal Studies teacher. I've forgotten my combination. I'm having a fricken bad-hair day and my face has so many pimples today, like a rocky road chocolate! So how's your day?' Sarah blurted unsympathetically and with a hint of sarcasm.

'Oh! Me? Well, I've had a great morning, sorry to say, and guess who's in my homeroom this year?' Leila said, grinning and displaying her wonderful teeth.

'Let me think … no! Don't tell me, it's Mark Bagher!'

'Shhh! Don't say his name so loud. Remember our pact last year to use abbreviations – it's CA, short for "Cute Arse", okay? Anyway, he looked directly into my eyes today and said, "Hi Leila." Did you hear that! He called me by my first name; I've still got the biggest crush on him. So do you think he likes me?'

'Leila! The only thing I can think about right now is getting my bloody locker open, so are you going to help?'

'Yeah, sure, let's go to the office,' Leila ordered, pulling Sarah's arm.

'That's the smartest suggestion I've heard all morning!' Sarah followed.

# Chapter Two

The love department was behind a locked door in the case of both Leila Mettar and Sarah. Both had strict parents from Arabic backgrounds and cruel, heartless brothers in common. Although Sarah was a smidgeon taller than Leila, they were labelled twins by fellow students when they really looked nothing alike, and had quite individual characteristics. Their personalities differed immensely. Sarah was agreeable by nature and popular. Leila, however, was firmly introverted, reserved and stubborn, equating to a negative attitude.

'Opposites attract', you may say; in Sarah's and Leila's case, this statement was a fact, although they seemed to get along, having mutual respect for one another – even if they were sometimes like conflicting magnets brought together.

At recess one afternoon, Sarah and Leila decided to sit on the oval. The sweet summer air frolicked against Sarah's cheeks; the fresh grassy smell of newly cut lawn brought warmth into their conversation as she confided in Leila. 'Have you seen Mr Fitzpatrick, the new English and Literature teacher?'

'I think the principal introduced him at assembly, but I didn't take much notice. Why?' Leila said, looking a little puzzled.

'There's something about him. I think he's really cute and he has beautiful eyes and an amazingly warm smile …'

Leila interrupted, 'You think your teacher is cute! Be careful! You know what they say about teacher/student relationships. They never work. Besides, I heard some guys saying the new teacher is an extrovert and may be gay.'

'Bloody hell, Leila! You're jumping the gun. I said he was cute and now you're making a quick assumption and judging the man. You don't even know him. Gosh, Leila, sometimes I wonder about you!' Sarah was angry but she brushed this statement off like tiny dust particles dispersing into the withering air.

Leila sighed. 'I'm sorry,' she said, humbled. 'I guess I just want to protect you!'

'Protect me! Is that what you call it? I'm seventeen, for crying out loud, and I get enough protection from my *loving* parents, who are always so controlling and interfering. If they continue, they may lose me as a daughter, and if you carry on like them, you may very well lose me as a friend!'

'Come on Sarah, no need to be so serious. Should I refresh your memory? How long have we known each other?'

'You're right, I'm sorry. I've had a bad day and I'm taking it out on you, but please, if I do mention a certain someone, let's call him NE for "Nice Eyes", okay?'

'Okay, Sarah, I will check out NE for you and give you a thorough report on his appearance!'

'Great! Now you're talking, friend!'

'Sarah, you didn't answer my question the other day. Do you think CA likes me?'

'Seriously, Leila, I do think he likes you, or at least is attracted to you.'

Leila sighed and breathed more easily, as if having been thrown a life buoy. Sarah was happy to see this. She wanted to see Leila happy, even if it meant lying to her. *That's what friends do,* Sarah thought. Make one another feel good about themselves, even when you don't quite believe what you're saying to be the whole truth and nothing but the truth. A little white lie can be handy at the best or worst of times.

'I've got to get to class. English with you-know-who,' said Sarah, glancing at her watch as she headed for her locker.

Leila virtually jogged beside her to keep up. 'So, you really think he's attracted to me?'

Sarah didn't make eye contact while retrieving her books. 'Ah, that's the bell. Gotta go. Catch you later!'

Sarah walked steadily into her class; she couldn't help but smile and made an effort to sit close to the front of the class this time.

Mr Fitz began discussing the first novel, *The Bell Jar*, and said he expected the whole class to have read it over the holidays. In fact, Sarah hadn't read it word for word. She just skimmed through the pages and read a little of the synopsis on the back cover. But she felt she could relate to Esther Greenwood, the central character of the novel, as she often felt trapped and depressed in her own life.

Mr Fitz mentioned how Esther becomes increasingly depressed and feels as though she's trapped under a metaphorical bell jar, which caused her to struggle for breath. Sarah couldn't help but draw similarities with feelings of suffocation from her controlling parents who, she had realised, intended to arrange her marriage and life partner.

'Sarah, would you like to start reading from *The Bell Jar*?' Mr Fitz said as he moved towards Sarah and touched the page of her novel with his index finger. Sarah noticed he wasn't wearing any rings and gathered he mustn't be married.

'Sure, Mr Fitz,' said Sarah, knowing that she would try her very best to read fluently and with expression; her love for acting would shine through, like a cloud with a silver lining. Sarah knew she wasn't the most attractive girl in the world or even in her classroom, but she did have an undeniable inner beauty like illuminate light on the gloomiest of days.

***

After class the same day, Sarah was talking to her group of friends in the locker area when she heard her name being called. She turned in surprise and hesitantly moved forward, peering over her shoulder to note her friend's reactions as if they had a bone to pick, which she happily ignored.

'Oh, Mr Fitz! How are you?' Sarah said almost automatically.

'Ah, Sarah, I just wanted to tell you that I was impressed with your reading in class today. You had the whole class captivated, maybe you should get into acting?'

'Thank you, Sir! As a matter of fact, I was involved in a little amateur theatre group in the past which has helped me a lot with confidence. It was called "Gangster Forty-five"! Pretty cool name, huh?'

'Yes, very impressive – well Sarah, keep up the good work. You're quite the little actress!' Mr Fitz said.

'Who are you calling "little"? Don't worry, I'll take that as a compliment … and, Sir, it was my pleasure.' Sarah giggled flirtatiously.

'Indeed, Sarah, keep up the wonderful work, the pleasure is ours, and you're an asset to my class!'

It was just the way he looked at her, the intensity of that sultry look in his eyes that made Sarah suddenly feel as if she were floating. A burning warmth filled her chest and fluttered inside her very being. She embraced this feeling, for she didn't want it to end and pondered for a moment: 'Was this what love feels like?' Because she yearned for it! And she wanted more, that's for sure. Sarah had never received much attention from the opposite sex and from this day forward she was love-struck, gobsmacked and smitten.

Sarah began to view life differently and saw beauty in things less apparent. She even observed while riding her bike one afternoon how extraordinary and most interesting the trees were: cedar, beech, fir and pine spruce. Their differing shades of green and claret. Sarah came to a sudden halt as she forced her pedal breaks into reverse. Stumbling across a spiralled brown-scaled pinecone, she picked up the seed case and examined it. There she evoked a memory of reading geometry text on ancient spirals and their winged seeds. This represented the winding journey inward, its bracts spiralling in a perfect Fibonacci sequence.

Bearing in mind the sacred universal patterns design of everything in our reality, Sarah noted her surroundings from a deeper perspective and took notice in things she would often take for granted, like 'Mother Nature'. *That which nature paints never fades.* Sarah knew this for sure and felt that memories in comparison would never leave her mind, further embedded inside her with each passing day.

Was this love, lust or perhaps just a crush? Sarah imagined this special something her and Mr Fitz shared together was like a plant – and the more they saw of one another, the more this plant was nourished and watered, thus thriving from their growing bond.

# Chapter Three

Life at the Basheer residence was very typical of a European household. Jamal took great pride in preparing traditional home-cooked Lebanese meals.

'Sarah, Dan … *yallah, yallah* lunch is ready!' said Jamal as she stirred the large age-old pot.

'Mum, smells great, what's cooking?' asked Sarah, as she dipped her finger carefully into the simmering pot and licked the aromatic flavours of Lebanese cuisine.

'It's yakni potato, *mah ris*,' said Jamal, meaning a beef and potato casserole with rice.

'You made my favourite, yummo! I'd love some of that!'

Before Sarah could reach for her bowl, Dan shoved her out of his way like a hungry hyena scavenging leftover lion kill. His mocking eyes roved over Sarah's face. 'Move out of my way, little girl, the *king* has to eat first!'

'Ouch! Mum, did you see that? You're such a bastard Dan, I really hate you!'

'*Dandino*! You wait until your father comma home to deala with you!' said Jamal, shaking but remaining calm enough to serve Dan a plate.

'*Shokran*, mama!' said Dan, after seating himself in front of his square electrical obsession box.

'Yeah, Dan, you wait until Dad comes home, you're really gonna get it big time, you loser!'

Dan argued with his mouth full. 'Oh, I'm so scared. My knees are shaking. The only person that's gonna get it is you, Sarah! After I tell Dad you've got a boyfriend and his name is … ah, let's see … perhaps Brad Tanker! Yes, ideal pair, the two of you, ha ha.'

'Shut up Dan! You bloody idiot! Why don't you go to your room like a normal sixteen year old and read? There's a book titled "Wankers and Losers, and Dan the living proof". You'll get yours one day. It's called karma — what goes around comes around!' Sarah announced forlorn.

'Such wise words from a baffled individual who thinks she's the female version of Confucius! Actually you look rather like him, although you need a good wax!' Dan laughed hysterically.

Sarah threw the nearest cushion without hesitation, aiming at Dan but missing — the cushion landed on Jamal's favourite ornamental vase, shattering it into a million pieces.

Before Sarah could begin to utter sincerest apologies to her mother, Dan couldn't help himself and smirked in his nasty way, looking directly at Sarah. 'You ought to borrow my book and you can change the title, even add your name! Ha! Let's talk about karma, mine or yours?'

Sarah, rather embarrassed, bent down to pick up the pieces. Jamal looked enraged. She was usually so very placid and kind, but when she got mad all hell would break loose. Jamal raised her hands and tugged at her hair. 'You both make me sick, oouff …where is your father? Look at my hands!' Jamal stretched her arms for her children to see her hands shaking uncontrollably. 'You both did this to me, you always make me sick.'

Sarah looked sympathetically at Jamal. Yet Dan turned a blind eye and said, 'Where is Dad, anyway? More than likely at his favourite place, "'the Holy Church", reading the Bible on daily doubles and the trifecta … ha,' Dan blurted, answering his own question.

'Shut up, Dan! That's all Mum wants to hear. As if she doesn't know that Dad's at the TAB.'

As Sarah said this, a familiar shuffle came from behind the front door and her father Marrouf appeared, more handsome than ever in Sarah's eyes. Tall and well-built with a wide forehead and dimple in the chin the devil within, as some would say. Although Marrouf was a heavy gambler, he had a generous spirit and could keep you captivated for hours with his storytelling flair.

'*Ahlan, ahlan!*' said Marrouf with a grin from ear to ear. He pulled out of his front shirt pocket (which usually contained a packet of Marlboro cigarettes) a handful of one hundred dollar notes. Marrouf flicked through them like a deck of playing cards.

'*Yih ya*, Marrouf! Where did you get all that money?' said Jamal as her mind raced around like a pack of wild horses.

'Jamal, you wouldn't believe it *habibti*. I had one hundred dollars left over from our pension money so I played in the Geelong Cup Sydney horse race. On the photo finish, Jamal! Thirty thousand dollars! I play the mixed race trifecta and now our dream to go see our family in Lebanon is in our hands … Here, Jamal! Take it! We will put it in the bank tomorrow.'

All was silent for a moment. Sarah felt frozen in time. Her throat felt sore and swollen, thoughts of emptiness and claustrophobia engulfing her almost immediately. She found an inner strength and words began to flow out of her, like a great waterfall in the Atlantic Ocean. 'Dad, I know this is a great day for you, and I should be happy for your winnings. But the thought of going to Lebanon is something I have really been dreading for a while. The truth is, I don't want to go and neither does Dan. You know, Dad! I want to finish year twelve, go to university and make something of my life. I don't want to be a housewife in a loveless marriage. I know very well what you and Mum are planning and I don't like it one little bit! I don't want to get married! This is the only reason you want to take us to Lebanon, it's not to view the touristic sights. Why don't you put the money to better use, maybe deposit on a nice house or something?'

Marrouf looked like a hawk as he glared at Sarah through grinded teeth. 'Sarah! That's enough silly talk. Lebanon is a beautiful country – you just wait and see. You and Dan are going to love it so much that you will never want to come back to Auzzie-tralia. Sarah, you can go to AUB, the American University of Beirut. It is number one university in Lebanon!' Marrouf raised his index finger and shook his hand as though addressing troops in an army camp.

Tears raced down Sarah's cheeks unnoticed as sadness sheathed her. Conversely, she remained poised, trying not to allow self-pity take hold of her.

'Okay already! Why do all our conversations have to revolve around Sarah and what she wants? Dad! What about me? Remember our bet that if you won over ten grand at the TAB, you would buy me a car. Don't even try to deny it, Dad! You know and you promised!'

Marrouf looked infuriated as he frowned at Dan. He looked at the ceiling, as if asking God to give him strength. 'Dan, I never promised you a car! Allah! We have raised selfish, selfish children that only think of themselves! We are going to Lebanon and that's final! I don't want to hear another word from the pair of you. Now Jamal, what did you cook? I'm very hungry.' Marrouf motioned towards the kitchen, his hand pressed firmly on his back as the throbbing pain transcended down his spine.

Sarah turned and headed towards her room. She wanted so desperately to argue some more, even lowering herself to begging and pleading with her father. Nonetheless she retreated to her room instead.

Sarah threw herself on her soft pink cerise doona, reached for her pillow and buried her face deeply into it. Her mind played tricks on her as she envisaged herself drowning at sea or falling off a cliff edge. She pressed the pillow further into her face until she couldn't take it anymore. The feeling of suffocation became unbearable. Sarah's blood began to boil; she cried until she felt she had no tears left to shed. Sarah grabbed her pen and notebook. She wrote her best when she was angry or upset.

> Selfish, selfish parents, only thinking of number one:
> themselves, and never taking any consideration in what their
> children want or need. I'm not talking material things, more
> like life in general. The path we wish to travel: shouldn't it be

our choice where in life we want to build a bridge, in order to discover our true essence and strengthen our stride? I have disgust and pity for those I despise – I don't feel I've lived or loved enough and I'm in a desperate struggle to find myself.

Who am I really? What do I want to achieve or accomplish in my life? I study till all hours of the morning for an exam or assignment – for what? To go overseas, namely Lebanon, a third-world country – and to marry some guy who claims to be my Romeo or knight in shining armour. Why on earth would he want me? Perhaps because of the word 'Visa' written across my forehead which will enable him to come to Australia and become a citizen of this lucky country!

Oh, Mr Fitz – how you are the light that shines on me ever so brightly. I am a flower and when you are near, I become alive with your warmth that nourishes and feeds my soul, bringing out the best in me, aiding a thriving bud to grow and blossom in a gloomy, weary world ...

Sarah was startled by a steady, heavy knock on her bedroom door. She quickly tucked her pen and notepad under her pillow.

'Sarah, *habibti*. May I come in?' Jamal didn't wait for a response and entered the room anyway, with Sarah's favourite mug detailing a half-horse, half-man with a bow and arrow depicting her star sign, Sagittarius. Jamal handed over the mug containing the familiar strong coffee aroma, which Sarah eagerly accepted with all angst aside. Jamal seated herself gently on her daughter's bed, placing her hand lightly on Sarah's back.

Jamal's motherly touch was always so comforting and warm. Even when Sarah was frustrated or upset, it seemed to work. As Sarah turned, sitting upright, she pulled her pillow ever so slightly behind her, to lessen the strain of her lower back. Before Sarah could utter a word, Jamal spoke in a soft and controlled tone.

'Sarah, I know you're upset and confused with all this ... your Father ... Lebanon ... but please listen. Lebanon is a beautiful country filled with beaches and ski resorts, rich in historical ruins, archaeology and sacred religious places – you know it was once called the Las Vegas of the Middle East, in the days when Lebanon was thriving? Then the civil war in 1975 destroyed and ruined the place we call home.

'Marrouf and I didn't want to raise children in an unstable country. We travelled to Australia in hope to give our children a better future, but Lebanon will always be in our hearts and minds. We can't deny our true roots, even though Australia has been very good to us, and the government looks after its people very well. What I'm trying to say is that your father and I want to show you and Dan where we were born. We have so much history and family. Your cousins, aunts and uncles all want to meet you. We want to show you what the national news fails to portray.

'Lebanon is a wonderful, charming country full of cedar trees, picturesque mountains and historic sites. We are Druze, tied to our land and based on a close-knit family structure. You must marry a Druze man to help our religion grow. This is the life – to marry and start your own family.'

Sarah rubbed her eyelids and could feel her tears welling up inside of her. 'Okay Mum, for crying out loud! I understand and I do want you and Dad to be proud of me. But I don't even really know what the Druze religion is – what is it? Who am I?'

Jamal laughed. 'I know, *habibti*. It's hard for you to understand, because we sent you to Catholic schools ...'

'That's true, and I believe in God and Jesus, good against evil – all that. All I know about the Druze is that they believe in God – only one God – I don't think the religion even follows a prophet.'

'Yes, they do follow holy ministers! The Druze believe that Hakim, the Incarnation of God, is not dead but absent, and will return to his people. They also believe in the potential of the release of divine aspects of the world, supernatural hierarchies, and in the transmigration of souls. The Druze are religiously divided into two groups. Those who master the secrets and education of the sect and who respect its codes of practice are stated as *uqqual* (the knowers), and are deemed the religious elite. Followers who are not entitled to know the inner secrets of Druze and who do not practice their religion are called *juhhal* (the ignorant).'

Jamal grasped the gold necklace around her neck. 'Sarah, see this chain and the round pendant? The five pointed star embodies the golden ratio, phi – as a symbol of temperance and living in moderation.'

'Yes mum, I know, it's the *kamsa hadood*, meaning the five-pointed star symbol.'

'The Druze star symbolises the five wise superior ministers or prophets, each with his quality.' Jamal continued, lowering her voice.

'Mum, what do the colours stand for?' Sarah said as she held the pendant in the palm of her hand.

'Each colour, Sarah, relates to a metaphysical power called *haad*, literally meaning limit, as in the parameters that separate humans from animals.

'Green represents "the mind", *al-akl*, the farmer and life.

'The colour red denotes "the soul", *an-nafs*, heart and love of humanity.

'Yellow suggests "the word", *al-kalima*, which is the purest form of expression of the truth, the sun and wheat.

'The colour blue, *as-sabik*, is for psychological influence of willpower, the sky and faith. And finally white, *al-tali*, is the awareness of *as-sabik*, where its power has emerged in the world of matter, air and purity. Resulting in the future and outcome.'

Jamal kissed Sarah's forehead. She proceeded to unclasp her chain and place it around Sarah's neck. 'Now *habibti*, I feel you should wear this as a reminder of your roots and our religion. It began as a derivate of Islam, based on the belief in the divinity of Fatimid Caliphate al-Hakim (985–1021), whom founded the Druze religion in Cairo, Egypt. Now you should get some rest – school tomorrow, remember?'

'How could I forget?' Sarah heaved a sigh; she considered the notion that the circle around the star was the *haad*, meaning limit. With that circumference in mind, were all the governing bodies and differing religious groups within that limit? Thus the colours could not form unison and become one. Could we arise awakening and speculate that all our souls are interconnected somehow?

Why not diversity of all religious belief systems co-existing in society? This is why we have patterns of division and violence.

Deeply fascinated and breathed a little easier knowing very well, she would see Mr Fitz in the morning. She made a pact with herself that she would take each day at a time and not delve too deeply into the future.

Sarah prayed that day, as she did often like a nightly ritual. Closing her eyes, she whispered, 'Dear God, thank you for everything you have given us, thank all the angels and saints, protect and guide me on the right path towards a better brighter future.' Sarah always felt strong after praying and repeating those unchanged words. She slept well that night.

# Chapter Four

Sarah crawled under the rock of shame at the very thought of her humble abode. A commission housing estate often labelled 'The Slums', it was a low socio-economic and disadvantaged community. However, for Sarah her most cherished memories were those growing up in this undesirable neighbourhood, which she tried desperately to keep secret.

Most houses were drab and uninteresting, constructed from concrete or weatherboard materials and bursting with red flesh leaf plum trees, pensioners and the unemployed 'dole bludgers' (as some would say).

Marrouf was titled an invalid pensioner from the time Sarah was eight years old. While she only had faint recollections of what her father did for work, she recalled Marrouf declaring his first job in Collingwood, called BBR–Repco – an automotive grinding company. There, he injured his back. Having ruptured his disc, Marrouf was granted the pension. He worked for a little while as a 'fruit delivery driver' and, not to forget, indulged in gambling when the need struck Marrouf.

Marrouf drove Sarah and Dan to and from school in his old 1978 olive green Ford Cortina – another one of Sarah's insecurities that her parents were unaware of.

Sarah awoke earlier than usual on this particular school day. Beside her bed lay, as usual, a neatly ironed uniform, with the bottle green blazer and striped tie all arranged in good order. Not to forget the clean knee-high socks nestled inside her school shoes, one of the many 'Jamal customs' for her only daughter's convenience.

Sarah was in and out of the shower in no time, with a quick dry and foundation to mask all imperfections. She was ready to conquer the world – or, in want of a better word, 'his' world.

'Dad! I'm ready, we're going to be late for school!' Sarah couldn't wait to vent her frustrations to Leila about her dad's winnings and travel plans to Lebanon.

'Sarah, I just finish my coffee! *Yallah, habibti*! We are going … where is Dan?' said Marrouf gently.

'He is still in the shower!' said Sarah with a sigh, glancing down at her watch.

Jamal approached with some toast and a cup of tea. 'Eat, Sarah, eat, don't go out on an empty stomach, this gives you energy!'

'I don't need energy! Dad, can we please go without Dan? He can walk to school – and besides, he needs to lose weight,' said Sarah abruptly.

'Oh Sarah! Why are you always horrible to your brother?' Jamal frowned and shook her head as she pushed the cup towards Sarah. 'Here, have some tea.'

Sarah turned away from her mother as Dan glided by and whisked the tea and toast out of Jamal's hands, as if he were on roller skates. 'Gee, thanks Ma! You shouldn't have. Really!'

Sarah looked at Dan with disgust and then at Jamal, who didn't seem fazed about what just occurred.

Marrouf grabbed his car keys while walking towards the door, and then turned to Jamal as if she were a lovely stream of light. 'Prepare yourself, Jamal. When I get back, we will go to the bank, and then maybe the flight centre to see how much tickets are to Lebanon.' Marrouf brushed his hand along Sarah's hair. 'You happy we are going to Lebanon, *habibti*?'

'Yes, extremely "happy" Dad, can't wait!' said Sarah pensively.

It took approximately a quarter of an hour to drive to school each morning, which always seemed like an endless trip. Thoughts circled Sarah's mind: thoughts of Lebanon, or rather fears of the unknown, Mr Fitz and her very existence that brought with it more uncertainty. At times Dan's irritating voice disturbed her train of thought and before she knew it she was at the school gates.

Sarah felt a cool northerly wind brush her face as she stepped out of the car. It was a lovely sunny day, blue sky and scattered clouds. Her eyes began to water, perhaps hay fever or symptoms of the flu coming on. As she gazed up at the school building, her eyes found the staff room window. Sarah imagined Mr Fitz standing there peering down at her, his warm smile engulfing her very being with feelings of comfort. A safe haven of peace and tranquillity.

'Hey Sarah! Are you crying? Ha, ha,' said Dan inquisitively with a slight cackle.

She shook her head and drew a deep breath. 'No, you moron! I've got hay fever.' Sarah wiped the corners of her eyes with her sleeve.

'Ooooh, touchy!' Dan added as he ran out of Sarah's sight.

Sarah saw Leila in the distance and waved to get her attention. In no time Leila was by her side, giggling and talking about CA – how he touched her shoulder and how she wasn't the slightest bit disinterested seeing CA with his new girlfriend, 'Miss Popular' Allyson Pier: blonde cascading hair, gorgeous luminous hazel eyes and exceptionally feminine. To Sarah's dismay, Allyson was Ms Binder's 'pet' as she was an A student and aced Legal Studies class. Allyson had all that every girl admired and boys dreamed about.

Sarah couldn't suppress feelings of resentment towards her parents as she felt in the land of limbo, not knowing what lay ahead for her future.

Leila nudged at Sarah's shoulder in displeasure. 'Sarah! What is with you? Why are you so preoccupied lately?' Leila's voice rasped angrily, frowning with a look of frustration.

'Oh, home shit … namely, parents! Bloody Dad won a large sum of money, and now we're going to "Lebo Land". I don't know if we're going tomorrow, in a couple of weeks or a few months from now, and knowing Dad he always does things on impulse. I'm really racking my brain over it.'

'Gee that hurts!' Leila went on. 'What about finishing year twelve, uni, me? Does this mean you're going for good? I'll have no one.' A million questions rushed through Leila's mind.

'Well, at least until they marry me off to some stranger.'

'Sarah, what are you saying, you can't go! Don't go – it's that simple.'

Sarah turned and pondered for a moment 'I wish life was that simple, but quite frankly it isn't! I feel like Mr Fitz is a tree, and I'm the frail leaf clinging on to him as my parents try to loosen my trembling hold. Remember Brad Tanker said once that "life's a bitch, then you die" – well, that's so true.'

'Brad said that after he asked you out and was rejected!' Leila reminded her in a fit of laughter, then quickly regained composure.

'Yeah well, I can't believe you think that's funny!' said Sarah, as they walked up the flight of stairs towards the locker bay, where she glimpsed at Mr Fitz talking to a female teacher. Sarah felt a little jealous but tried to ignore this emotion, hoping that it was just friendly conversation. Amidst the good and wise thoughts, warped morose voices echoed – *Perhaps he's dating her?*

*You're too young for him.*
*You're only his student.*
*Nothing can ever happen between you.*
*You don't drive a car.*
*You're not independent.*
*How could you introduce him to your parents?*
*They will never accept him, nor will his folks.*
*He will be ashamed of where you live.*
*You're a poor, worthless child!*

This went on and on, revolving around in her mind, tormenting Sarah as treacherous thoughts encased her soul. She shuddered for a moment, took a long deep breath and released slowly with a strong sigh of relief.

'Sarah! Are you okay? You're sweating – you look quite sick!' Leila said as she wiped Sarah's brow with the palm of her hand, then flicked her wrist in order to wipe away any remaining residue. 'Yuck! I think you need some water.'

If looks could kill, Leila would have been dead as Sarah gave her the 'evil eye'. 'So you think I look sick? Just be honest and say I look shit. Cause that's what you mean, isn't it? When people say, "You look unwell today," they really mean, "You look really bad today!"'

'Oh Sarah, why do you always twist my words? I do worry about you.' Leila eyed her watch. 'Look at the time, you'd better get to Legal Studies class quick or Ms Binder will have you in a bind.'

Sarah resumed classes as usual and on many occasions through Legal Studies, Ms Binder caught Sarah dawdling and scribbling on paper. On this occasion Sarah was writing a poem to someone in particular.

With you in my mind and dreams, I can cast aside the fears of my life now with you in it. High school crush some would say, but it's much deeper and intense. Your deep blue eyes captured mine, at moments when time stood still.

I'm not willing to brush this off as lust.

Like two pieces of celestial dust – let us live and linger.

Deep within ... deep within, the spark will never die. Heartfelt emotions running through me.

I want to reach out and grasp hold of you, if only for a minute.

Deep within and within the deep I'm drowning at a deadly pace.

Oh Mr Fitz, out of all the high schools why did you have to waltz into mine?

Downing in sorrow.

Drowning in pity.

Drowning in visions of you.

So deep, deeper. Breathless. How can I escape these pent-up feelings? Throw a life buoy out to sea and save me from reality.

Sarah dropped her pen at the sound of Ms Binders' ear-splitting voice 'Ms Basheer, Wake up young lady! Do you want to continue reading the rest of the paragraph, which Allyson thoughtfully started?'

'Ahhhh …' Sarah began to read a paragraph at random, which proved incorrect.

Ms Binder frowned. 'Just as I suspected! You weren't paying attention, were you young lady?' She then turned to Allyson and said with a smile, 'Thank you, Allyson, you may continue reading.'

Sarah was embarrassed, her face felt warm and flushed. She had a very severe case of 'Mondayitis'. Not a great start to Legal Studies class, but she knew very well what the rest of the year had in store for her and getting into law may not have been one of them.

Sarah resumed classes as usual such as Reasoning and Data (Mathematics), Religious Education and Economics and looked forward to English and Literature.

Literature in particular included reciting poems and sonnets, which Sarah loved and looked forward to. Mr Fitz knew plenty about poetry: analysing, dissecting poems and shredding apart sentences and their meanings – what the poet is attempting to depict.

In Sarah's eyes, Mr Fitz had profuse brilliance in every way. His intelligence drew her closer, like a fish being enticed by fisherman's bait. She loved it when she felt his eyes on her when she looked away; the more she got, the more she wanted, even though she knew her feelings were dangerous if made public.

Sarah sought to find out everything about him – his history, where he grew up, essentially his past, present and future. She wanted to be part of him in every way. Sarah knew deep down how he felt for her too, such a strong connection with no need for words or communication; she knew he was attracted to her both physically and mentally. How he gazed into her eyes with longing.

He said her work had 'spark' – did he mean 'they' shared a spark together?

Mr Fitz had a habit of saying things to Sarah indirectly, and didn't want to make his affections 'obvious' in fear of losing his job. If his feelings were indeed made evident, Mr Fitz would be branded the laughing stock of the school. Sarah couldn't have that weighing on her conscience, for she too could not express openly how she felt, even to Mr Fitz – Spencer – himself.

Leila swore never utter a word to a soul. Sarah trusted her best friend, and that her secret lay feebly safe in a whirlwind of emotion.

# Chapter Five

The arrival of yet another sun-kissed day urged Sarah and Leila to walk to the oval at school recess.

Sarah felt a crisp edge to the air and the smell of a freshly cut lawn. Trees budding and some in blossom, offering rise to childhood memories. Sarah recalled Marrouf and Jamal gardening and digging a veggie patch in their back garden that had thrived. Lebanese parsley for Mum's famous tabouli, thyme, rosemary, basil, cherry tomatoes, fresh green aromatic mint, sweet strawberries and the much loved 'aspirin' lemon tree. Jamal called their lemon tree 'aspirin' as whenever one of her family had a headache, she would squeeze lemon juice to mix with water, sugar and a dash of rose water – after drinking this mixture, the migraine would disappear. Though Sarah quickly reminded herself she was still upset with her parents, and soon the fresh flavoursome scent dispelled.

Leila exclaimed to Sarah how CA, Allyson Pier and a few boys were playing footy on the oval. Sarah, being the more outgoing of the pair, built up the courage and asked Allyson if they could join them.

'Sure, go for it!' said Allyson as she flicked her golden locks and passed the football to Sarah. She noticed Mr Fitz looking in her direction from the other side of the oval.

Sarah turned. 'Leila! Is that Mr Fitz looking at us? Perhaps I should go over and talk to him.'

'No, let's stay please! This is heaps fun and CA keeps looking at me! See?' Her face flushed pink.

Sarah kicked the footy and with it her shoe hovered in mid-air before dropping at an alarming rate, like an aircraft descending for landing. As she was hopping towards it with immense awkwardness and humiliation, Mr Fitz approached (shoe in hand, grin on face). 'Oh, thanks Mr Fitz, I owe you one.'

'That's quite all right! You seem to be flustered. You know something? Don't be so hard on yourself, these embarrassing moments happen to the best of us.'

'Yeah, well, some people have all the luck!' As Sarah said this, the football was headed in his direction and right for his head. 'Watch out!' Sarah bellowed, pushing Mr Fitz out of the ball's firing line.

'Gee, thanks! Now I owe you one.'

'Now you owe me two!' she said, again nudging him to move yet a second time.

'Yes, indeed I do!'

At this stage Sarah noticed CA and a few other boys staring at them curiously, wondering what Mr Fitz was doing on the oval, talking to Sarah. She knew they purposely aimed the ball at Mr Fitz, in order to make a mockery of the situation.

She was thrilled she was able to help him, as the excitement of just being near him was enough. And she felt the feeling was mutual.

Sarah lost sight of Leila as she walked back to class, with Mr Fitz by her side chatting about some assignment that was due; she knew he wanted to make any excuse to exchange words.

Mr Fitz had invited his Literature students to the movies. Sarah felt he intended to sit next to her in the movie theatre, but Celine Achen seized the seat next to him so quickly, as if playing musical chairs. Sarah was left sitting two seats down from Mr Fitz. She noticed Celine lift her legs and rest them on the seat in front of her. She certainly had a thing for Mr Fitz and wanted to show off her legs, which Sarah thought was so disrespectful.

Celine was of German descent, a tawny colour tone with large beady dark eyes and a huge disfigured nose. She had a thin and lanky body, hardly attractive, and would often drag or slur her words. Celine would say, 'Ooooh Sarah, yoooou liiike Mr Fitz don't you? Does he make you go weak at the kneeees?' More like a statement than a question. Sarah would ignore her, as she thought of Celine like a housefly, wishing at times she had a flyswatter.

On many an occasion at recess or lunchtime, Sarah would go to the library. Mr Fitz would mysteriously be there, like he was stalking her every move. Sarah felt flattered as he watched her chatting to classmates and purposely flirting with boys to make him jealous.

An incident and flashback occurred when both herself and Celine were asking Mr Fitz a question – he ignored Celine, brushing her off to give Sarah his full and utmost attention as per usual.

Was it pure coincidence or simply by chance that Mr Fitz was there on the day of Sarah's year twelve group photo? He was standing nearby, watching as the photographer captured snapshots simultaneously. Similarly, he was at the school 'Sock Hop' (which was a fancy dress disco with few teachers supervising the night). Mr Fitz was wearing the Phantom of the Opera mask and suit, looking more handsome than ever.

Not forgetting the day he peered over Sarah's shoulder while she was writing an informative piece on 'How to attract the opposite sex'. She'd stated that eye contact was the 'key' – and funnily enough Mr Fitz gave her more eye interaction than usual! Or the time Nicole, a fellow classmate, was given her essay after correction, finding at the bottom of the page where Mr Fitz would state his final comment and grading was Sarah's name instead of Nicole. *How weird*, Sarah reflected. Nicole was quick to point this out to Mr Fitz, whom scribbled Sarah's name out quickly and wrote 'NICOLE' in bold.

'Can you believe that Mr Fitz got my work mixed up with yours? Even writing your name, Sarah! Look at my writing style, it's nothing like yours!' Nicole pondered, pointing out a clear silly mistake for a teacher to make.

Sarah's name seemed imprinted and fixed in his mind and Mr Fitz couldn't stop thinking about her, especially when he wasn't at work, he would find himself reiterating events during his busy working day week. Particularly Sarah being the central component in his thinking span. He knew so much about her, perhaps more than she knew herself.

Sarah's love of acting and singing, that she was of Lebanese descent, her interest in law, that she was witty having a good sense of humour and most striking of all the fact she was a little paranoid and did not know how beautiful she really was. He loved all this about her and feasibly when Jamal said that one's imperfections made you the unique person that you are, her mother hit the nail on the head spot on, as indeed she was right!

# Chapter Six

Sarah heard the phone's piercing tenor bell from her bedroom as she lay on her bed listening to the best of Sir Elton John. Sarah loved Elton's lyrics, full of substance and love, in particular, 'Your Song'.

Jamal poked her head around the door. 'Sarah! The phone, it's for you! Put the music lower, your dad is sleeping, okay!'

'Alrighty then Mum, I'm getting up.' Sarah stretched her legs, slipped on her floral granny slippers and yawned, sighing glumly. 'Yes Leila, I'm coming.'

Leila would call Sarah religiously everyday straight after school. Sarah picked up the phone and held it gently to her ear. 'Hello Leila!' Sarah expressed shrewdly.

'Hi, how are you?' Leila didn't stop there, jumping right into complaining about other students. 'I mean, the boys are so cruel and immature in our year level … except for CA of course. He's so hot, don't you think? You better not, he's mine – or will be. I don't even know where he was? Okay, okay, with Allyson I know, but do you think he likes me? Now be serious, what do you think really? Do you think he thinks I'm attractive? In what way do you think? Does he see me as a potential girlfriend?'

Sarah tried hard to interrupt but couldn't get a word in edgewise. She held the receiver away from her ear now as Leila babbled on and on about CA and other things. While she loved Leila all the same, she couldn't handle her self-absorbed obsessive behaviour. 'Leila, Leila, I have to go! Dad has to use the phone sorry, and he is getting really agro at me. Don't worry we'll talk at school tomorrow, okay? Love ya babes!'

'But Sarah! I didn't have a chance to tell you about …'

Before Leila could continue Sarah put down the receiver, as much as it hurt her. She felt that there were serious issues to discuss with her parents about the dreaded foreseeable travel plans to Lebanon.

Sarah sauntered as if walking on eggshells to the living room, where she observed the usual behaviour of Dan as his eyes were transfixed on the television as he watched *Beverly Hills 90210*: all oversized blazers and floral patterns, cut off Levi's jean shorts and lace bandage dresses, loose knit sweaters and light denim and leather combinations.

Marrouf was assisting Jamal pan fry quails for dinner in the kitchen, squeezing lemons and garlic to pour over the succulent meal, sage and rosemary to enhance flavour.

Jamal turned to Sarah, her smile faint. 'Sarah, go outside please and collect a bunch of parsley and mint leaves for our tabouli! It will go lovely with the quails, but don't forget to put on a jumper.'

Sarah ignored the 'jumper' part and grinned. 'Okay Mum, no probs.'

Sarah walked out to the vegie patch in the back garden; she felt the icy wind as its sharpness cut through her bones like icicles plying through her skin, but this didn't deter her as she casually picked the parsley. Marrouf followed with Jamal's seagrass oval basket and began helping Sarah bunch together the strong scented parsley and put it in the hamper.

'Dad, I was just wondering, have you booked the tickets for Lebanon yet?'

'As a matter of fact, your mum and I booked our tickets on the day we went to the Arab travel agent. I thought I told you, a day after my beautiful lucky Sydney race win! So we're going in the middle of December, just before Christmas. Oh Sarah *habibti*, I can smell it now, smoking the Arghileh water pipe.'

'Is that like what the Hookah-Smoking Caterpillar was smoking in Lewis Carroll's *Alice in Wonderland*?'

'Oh yes, Sarah, I think you are a genius *habibti*! The Arghileh mixture is 15% tobacco, you know. Mixed with honey, fruits and chemical additives that are cooked and fermented. Better than Marlboro, *ya habibti* … Ahhh, Lebanon!' Marrouf looked up at the sky with a daydream stare. 'Sitting on the Manara Roauchi, admiring the view of the Pigeon Rocks, the two limestone rock formations which are wondrous to the human eye … When I arrive I want to kiss the ground and the dirt under my feet,' pined Marrouf.

*Yuck, how disgusting!* Sarah let her dad immerse himself in happy and tranquil thoughts about Lebanon, until finally she couldn't contain herself and blurted, 'Dad, that's too soon! It's not the right time, what if I get into university and exams are coming soon, they're just a few months away … Dad, Dad, just listen.'

'When in life is it the right time? God gave us the money so we make the time. We already discussed your options for university in Lebanon. Don't worry too much, Sarah *habibti*, you will get a headache and your mum will be squeezing lemons in no time, I promise you that! Ha ha …' Marrouf's belly began to wobble as he chuckled the way Sarah imagined Santa Claus would. 'Let's go inside. I could eat a horse, you know, and we better get chopping that parsley before the quails get cold.'

'Yeah Dad, I guess you're right – we can't stop the inevitable!' Sarah said, at risk of sounding too maudlin.

After dinner Sarah thought about the invitation she received at school earlier, pushing aside thoughts of Lebanon. Sarah felt she would strike up the courage and opportunity to ask about the birthday invite to Allyson's party, even though it was two weeks away, giving her parents ample time to ponder the thought and allow her to go to the coolest party ever. Receiving an invite from the most popular group at school was not only rewarding, but also satisfying to say the least as Sarah was slowly working her way up the social ladder at school.

'Mum, dinner was delicious, I really enjoyed that!' Sarah gathered the plates and put them in the sink as she began to wash them. 'I was invited to Allyson's 18th birthday party today and it's in a couple of weeks' time, can I go please?'

'You know how your dad feels about parties; he doesn't like you to go. It's not you we don't trust, it's the other people we don't trust.'

Whenever Sarah would ask her parents to go anywhere she would hear that precise sentence: 'It's the people we don't trust' … Sarah didn't know why she even bothered asking her parents to go anywhere. Jamal would often say 'We are Druze! We don't have boyfriend. When you grow up you have to marry Druze man to help our religion grow, you be good girl. No party, no boyfriend, no sleepover slumber party and no school camping! *But we trust you Sarah!*'

To Sarah's dismay, double standards applied for 'Druze boys' as Dan was allowed to go to parties, movies and sleepovers with friends. Marrouf would often joke cordially about Dan having a girlfriend. 'Hey *ya* Dandino, how many girlfriends this week eh?' If Sarah even uttered the word boyfriend around her dad, he was sure to get out his shotguns!

Sarah began to consolidate a plan: perhaps if she slept over at Leila's house, they could go to Allyson's party! Leila's parents weren't strict and allowed Leila a little freedom. They were Palestinian and could speak fluent Arabic. Marrouf and Jamal permitted Sarah's friendship with Leila because of this and may consent to Sarah sleeping over for one night. If by chance all went well, Sarah would go to the party and pray her parents wouldn't make contact with Leila's house on the night or ask any questions. That was the risk Sarah was willing to take.

# Chapter Seven

Legal Studies class the following day started out with Ms Binder licking her bottom lip, as she did when she was trying to make a point. She drew her spectacles below her dilated pupils. 'Class, we all know that there are loopholes in the justice system! Now I ask you, what is just? What does the term "just" mean?'

As soon as Sarah heard the word 'just' she fell into a trance and couldn't stop thinking how unjust her parents had been for the past seventeen years of her life. Sarah would often ask herself why 'Auzzie' parents were so cool and allowed their children to go out with friends to parties and social events. Having boundaries was one thing, but being so strict to the point of suffocating your child by wrapping them in cotton wool was a drastic measure in her eyes.

Sarah once heard a wise old friend say that a teenager is like a bar of soap: hold on to it too tightly and it will simply slip through your fingers. Be firm but gentle and it won't slither out of your grasp. Gradually Sarah began to feel the only alternative in her existence was to rebel and lie in order to get what she wanted or the freedom she desired.

Then there was 'Spencer' – as shadow cannot exist without light, he was the one person who could make her life complete and utterly perfect, the bright yang to Sarah's dark yin. Life was only worth living if he was in it. Indeed, Spencer was part of her life – at least for the two hours of classes per day, five days a week. Sarah missed him immensely on weekends and school holidays. Like the earth yearns for the sun's embrace. Spencer's absence equated to acid rain, as Sarah envisaged blackened trees resembling giant skeletons in the Black Forest.

Legal Studies ended the same way it had started, and as usual Sarah daydreamed her way through all classes with the exception of Spencer's lessons. She found herself sniffing and rubbing her nose to the point it became like a leaking tap that needed the attention of a plumber.

Spencer stretched out his hand in a lovely gesture. 'Sarah, would you like to use my handkerchief?'

Sarah felt embarrassed; she suspected Spencer saw her wiping her nose with the end of her sleeve. Sarah blushed, eyes on the floor, and shook her head. 'No thank you, Mr Fitz.'

'Don't worry Sarah, I haven't used it!'

'Oh I believe you Sir, but I'm fine really.' Sarah said hesitantly. She didn't know why she didn't accept his clean, neatly folded hanky; perhaps her shyness got the better of her. When Sarah wasn't acting, she couldn't hide behind the storybook character to escape her reality.

At recess, Leila and Sarah discussed Allyson's upcoming party. 'So Sarah, don't keep me in suspense! Are you going to Allyson's party or not?' Leila asked, biting her lower lip and expecting the usual negative answer.

Sarah had a twinkle in her eye. 'I've been thinking, how about I sleep over your place on the night and we go from there? You see, we devise a plan so that my parents never find out and everybody is happy. It's a win/win situation and no one gets hurt! We get to go to the party of a lifetime, you get to see CA, my parents are happy thinking I'm snug in my bed and a good "Druze girl" …'

'Ahh Sarah, I don't know …' Leila frowned and a look of worry masked her face. 'I think there is something you're missing, in particular somebody younger than you living under your roof, whom hates you having an inkling of freedom and despises your very existence!'

'I have crossed my "T"'s and dotted all my "I"'s, lovely Leila. Mayday, Mayday …Check Dan! All sorted I bribed Dan with a little cash I saved from doing little chores for some elderly in our local community granny flats.' Sarah pointed her thumbs towards herself and smiled infectiously. 'I've only given Dan a quarter of one hundred buckaroos! Just in case he stumbles and lets the cat out of the bag. If all goes well to plan he will pocket the rest accompanied with a big juicy kiss.'

'Definitely not the latter! Oh Sarah, you never cease to amaze me. I honestly hope you get away with this as I would hate for your master plan to turn sour, where your parents quickly send you skyrocketing to Lebanon on a one way ticket.'

'Well, we will soon find out. Until then I just want to enjoy the moment, seize the day, grab the bull by the horns! You know what I mean.'

'Yes Sarah, I know the drill! Stick a fork in me, I'm done.'

'I will ask my parents tonight, beg them if I have to. Don't worry, I'm going to that party if sleeping over your place is my final passage to freedom!'

***

The evening grew dark and gloomy as forceful gusts of wind stretched high and wide. Dan played obsessively on his Nintendo, unaware of the stormy weather outside. Sarah thought if there were an earthquake or the roof blew off their house, Dan would still be clenching his remote control and pushing those damn buttons. Marrouf was in the lounge room watching an Arabic movie, which Sarah gathered was an Adel Imam flick. Marrouf was quite fond of this comedian and Sarah knew him well, growing up with her dad's constant babbling about Lebanese (or in this case, Egyptian) reputable actors. Jamal occupied herself in the kitchen, keeping busy with household chores, not once taking a breather to stretch her legs or watch a movie with Marrouf.

Sarah grabbed this opportunity to pop the big question. 'So Dad! I love this part – Adel Imam is so hilarious, his character really draws you in and you have no choice but to like the guy, and his looks grow on you. The more I watch his movies and comedies the more I find him attractive, but I guess you're a guy so never mind.' Sarah felt embarrassed and giggled nervously.

'Sarah *habibti*, you're right, but the man is very talented and all Arabs vouch for that. He is a lot like Jerry Lewis: funny, gifted and popular.'

Sarah twisted in her seat, flicked her hair. 'Dad, Leila asked if I could sleep over her place. Seeing as I'm not allowed to go to Allyson's party … you know Leila's parents and it will only be for one night, we're gonna watch movies and eat popcorn!'

'Popcorn and movies – yes, why not?'

Sarah could not believe her ears, and immense joy filled her entirety. How could such a hard question be so simple once said? She'd racked her brain for a week thinking about what to say, picking and dissecting the right words.

Today it happened! The word she was waiting to hear her whole life, *'yes'* and twice-in one sentence, quite baffling she reflected.

Sarah was indeed in heaven, flying and fluttering her wings. Every part of her being oddly desired to hug Dan at this moment – but opted to kiss Marrouf on the cheek instead, which was much more rewarding.

# Chapter Eight

Leila resided in a lovely, upper class suburb in her double-storey home overlooking a lovely picturesque view. Sarah enjoyed her stay at Leila's, in particular on this day as it was not only a sleepover, but also Allyson's party!

'What are you going to wear, Sarah? Show me!' Leila grabbed Sarah's bag and forcefully unzipped it to recover the items, probing each garment separately. 'Ooh so sexy Sarah, black pleated skirt, lacy black patterned singlet top – not see-through, so classy – and look at those platform shoes! Who are you trying to impress?'

'Nobody!' Sarah said defensively. 'You know whom I like, no one can take his place.'

'He's not your boyfriend, you know.'

'And CA is not yours! I don't see you keeping your options open.'

'I would if Prince Charming came along, but no such offers as yet.'

'Okay, so we're in the same old shipwreck, but who cares? Now let's eat! Your mum's cooking is great! Then we'll get dressed.'

'Cool, sounds like a plan to me, let's hope your other master plan works!'

'All in good time, my dear, all in good time.'

Sarah's strategy did go according to her master plan. Leila even went to the extent of taking the phone slightly off the receiver, hoping no family members would use the phone – thus, no calls could connect.

Upon arrival at Allyson's party, Sarah felt a profound excitement like a young child taking their first baby steps. Sarah was walking for the first time into the freedom she so relished. Loud music, loads of hotties, alcohol aplenty and, best of all, no adults. Sarah and Leila began dancing at once, dismissing wishing Allyson a happy birthday and neglecting to buy her a present as the pre-party planning took over their thoughts.

Sarah couldn't stop thinking about Spencer and how great the party would have been if he were present; he may not have fit in, she deliberated, but for her sake only his presence would have made everything worthwhile.

Leila was thinking about CA; she had spotted him playing pool with a group of friends. She struck up the courage go over towards her target, dragging Sarah along and attempting to blend and intermingle. Leila whispered, 'CA is such a pool shark! Look at those strong, muscular arms.'

Sarah interrupted under her breath, 'I don't care! Besides, if Allyson sees you she won't be happy you're eyeing out her man!' Sarah pulled Leila's arm and proceeded to the finger food and beverages, which were more heart-warming, considering Sarah felt a little depressed as her mind travelled with visions of Spencer.

She later walked outside the building to get some fresh air. There she saw a group of youths drinking alcohol on the bitumen and Sarah found herself drawn in the midst of all this pandemonium, drinking from a number of shared bottles. Sarah knew very well what she was doing was wrong and not good for her health. *Dying brain cells – or just lack thereof,* she thought. But for a moment, no more, that initial feeling of soothing warmth ran through her, turning like a venomous snake sliding and injecting small rapid incisions down her throat. The burning sensation scorched her insides and her chest felt numb. Sarah felt a guilty rush of happiness and unwanted bouts of laughter.

Sarah overheard hysterical cries and dug in closer amongst the crowd, observing a clearly intoxicated girl say as she groped her breasts and sobbed as she sat on the asphalt, 'Why do guys just want me for these things? I hate them; I'm getting a breast reduction! Why can't they just like me for me?'

Leila grabbed Sarah's shoulder, turning her so they faced each other, and glared at Sarah. 'What did you drink? Do you even know what they bloody put in those bottles? I'll tell you! They mix every alcoholic drink in the book and God only knows what else. I thought you were smarter!' Leila grabbed Sarah, trying to lead her back into the hall.

Sarah turned to face the road and yelled at the top of her lungs 'Mr Fitz … I love you!'

'Shhh, be quiet, you idiot! Everyone can hear you! Now shut up and come inside,' Leila exclaimed in horror.

Brad Tanker appeared from the distance. 'Is Saa … rah drunk? Le … let me he … elp her.' He held Sarah's hand, while the other was firmly placed on her back.

He guided her as Leila looked in disbelief, yet allowed him take her anyway as Sarah seemed happy enough. Leila lurked behind, keeping an unyielding eye on Sarah.

*Brad's the perfect gentleman*, Sarah thought as he seated her on a chair near the dance floor and told her to stay put, as he procured a glass of water.

'The … there you go princ …ess,' said Brad with a smile.

Sarah felt her eyes beginning to get heavy and her tummy queasy.

Brad lent forward. 'I really want to kiss you right now Sarah,' he whispered without stuttering and led her, unwillingly, on to the dance floor. He pressed her in towards him and passionately kissed her, grasping her face ever so tenderly, as if she was the last and most fragile candle on earth where there was no light. He felt he mustn't allow the flame burn out for the sake of her life and his own. It was evident how fond Brad was of Sarah. Yet Sarah had no feelings for Brad except that of pity fused with repulse, as she tasted a mixture of tobacco, alcohol and dry retch.

Leila yelled as loud as her voice could project over the music as she pulled Brad off Sarah. 'What do you think you're doing? Sarah's drunk, you idiot, and you want to take advantage of her!' Leila glanced around and noticed people giggling and amused, as seeing Brad with anything, let alone a human being, was something nobody could fathom.

'I think I'm gonna be sick.' Sarah put both hands on her mouth and Leila ran her to the bathroom.

'Oh my God, Sarah! You're so lucky your parents aren't picking you up tonight, and I hope my dad doesn't suspect you've been drinking!' Leila wiped Sarah's mouth with some scrunched up toilet paper. 'There you go, but I think you should wash your face, or at least your mouth, your breath stinks.'

'Get off me you fucken psycho!' Sarah shoved Leila to one side, not realising her own strength.

'As usual, just trying to help – a simple thank you wouldn't go astray. I should have let plump old Brad do what he wanted with you! Shit, look at the time – it's 11.30. My dad will be here in less than half an hour cause my curfew is at midnight usually.'

Sarah looked at herself in the mirror, hardly recognising the ugly vision reflected, and interrupted with, 'Well, lucky you! I feel like shit, let's get out of this puke room!'

As Leila led Sarah and heaved open the heavy cubicle door, she couldn't believe what she saw – and as much as Leila prayed her eyes were deceiving her, like some kind of hallucination, her head screamed *reckoning* from the beastly truth standing motionless and headstrong before her very eyes. Like a ravaged madman, Marrouf was present at Allyson's party, looking like he had seen a ghost.

Sarah caught her dad's eyes and with that, he jolted his body forward. He clutched her arm, slapping her face so hard that the entire room shook in bitter cold silence. '*Yallah*, Sarah! Movies and popcorn, eh? Walk!' Marrouf made a gesture as if spitting on the ground – *ptih* – as he did when he was angry. He then pointed at Leila. 'You, too, come with me.'

Sarah felt a salty, metallic taste in her mouth and gathered it must be blood as it tricked down the nape of her neck. Marrouf began to roar every insulting name in the Arabic book at her. She had never felt so humiliated in all her life! She asked herself, was that the price of freedom? Was it all worth it? She didn't care how Marrouf found out or how he came to be at the party that night. Her plan had fizzled out.

The only thing Sarah couldn't erase from her mind was her sheer embarrassment. How could she face everyone at school? Sarah wished there was no such place as school at that moment. Whatever punishment Marrouf had in store for her, it was punishment enough having to face everybody at school; kissing Brad, although one-sided, would scar the rest of her school life – or what was left of it.

Sarah and Leila sat together in the back passenger seats of Marrouf's car. They didn't exchange one word to each other, listening in silence at Marrouf's taunts for the rest of their journey. 'We put our trust in our children and this is what Jamal and I get in return, a kick up the bum. We should have raised you in Lebanon! You stupid! You don't think! You thought you could outsmart us, eh? Lies, lies! You see all boys and girls drinking, smoking, rolling around outside! Well, I see. I see everything. I thought you good girl! But just stupid!'

Sarah's jaw and upper cheek still throbbed with pain from one single lashing which felt like a thousand, as Marrouf unceasingly ranted and raged. Perhaps her guilt weighed on her pain as Leila comforted her. Sarah's eyes drew heavy as she stared at passing traffic lights and swerving car signals. She wished she were home, sleeping soundly in her bed, and dreaded the fact that Leila had to be dropped off at the next destination.

# Chapter Nine

The following morning, Sarah heard the early birds chirping their morning recital as she lay in her bed dreading what day it was and how she fell into this predicament. Hoping it was not a school day.

She had a severe headache and nausea. Her first hangover, she believed, and the ugly reality of the morning after plagued her body inside and out.

Sarah didn't feel the need to get out of her warm bed, nor did she want to leave the comfort of her room. She felt immobile as she lay there, deducing what kind of mess she was in. Had this event sparked the arrival of their beloved trip to Lebanon to come sooner rather than later? She hoped not.

Jamal called from the other room, '*Yallah* Sarah, wake up! It's almost 11.00, come help me hang out the washing.'

Sarah stretched her whole body and realised it must be Sunday; she was relieved but at the same time anxious, as facing her parents about the night before would be unbearable to say the least. Sarah grabbed a towel and ducked into the bathroom to have a quick shower. She looked in the mirror, saw the baggy dark shadows under her eyes and felt sick to the stomach, thinking how stupid she was for drinking what may have proved to be a toxic mix. Sarah didn't want to face anyone; she ran the water until the hot steam dispersed throughout the small room.

Sarah felt relief as the warm water pelted, massaging her back and shoulders as her muscles loosened. Sarah was still a little worried at the thought of confronting her parents; nevertheless, after putting on some comfortable clothing, she walked to the laundry and began helping Jamal, gathering one wash load after another.

'I am very angry with you, Sarah! I can't even look at you – your father doesn't want to look at or speak to you. There is one thing your father and I know for sure: we are going to Lebanon as soon as possible, and for good! Mark my words, we are not coming back! We are happy because we managed to get an earlier flight. That is the best for you and Dan to be raised with good, decent boys and girls. Your grandmother used to say, god rest her soul, if you put one good apple in amongst bad, mouldy apples, that one good apple will soon get rotten and deteriorate! Just like you, if you mix with imbeciles who are up to no good. You know what I mean, Sarah – it is for the best!'

'Okay Mum. So what did Dad say about Lebanon, when are we going exactly?'

'In less than four weeks. I've already started packing your and Dan's clothes.' Jamal smiled and Sarah felt as though her mother was mocking her as she began humming an Arabic oldie.

Sarah thought immediately about Spencer and how she couldn't possibly leave him when nothing had even started. Sarah wanted to argue with her mum, but knew well enough she was in too deep with her parents already. Uttering any words would only be digging a deeper hole for her grave.

Sarah began to estimate how much time she had left of school and if she would complete all her exams – and she had to verify when the school formal would be held. She hoped her parents would have the heart to let her go to the most important event (teacher supervised) of school history, the formal – she couldn't wait to get all dressed up for Spencer.

'Sarah!' yelled Marrouf as he walked by, her stopping so abruptly and frightening her that she jumped out of her skin. 'What in Allah's name are you thinking about? A boy? Or another way to lie to go to a drinking, rolling around the streets party, eh?' Marrouf made a silly gesture in the air with his hand as if he had some kind of body spasm.

'No, Dad! I was just thinking … Mum said …'

Marrouf cut Sarah off before she could even begin to defend her case; Sarah felt he had no trust or empathy for her whatsoever. Sarah missed the friendship and trust she built with Marrouf and wondered how on earth she could win that back. What could she possibly do to revive her relationship with her father? At this moment in time she knew this couldn't be possible, but time did play an important role – even though she didn't have much of it left. She hoped Allyson's party would be a distant blurry memory. Sarah psyched herself for all the upcoming events in her life, including the ones she'd rather not think about. Dan was the last person she wanted to talk to. Keeping her distance from him and the remainder of the family, she resorted to her hiding place and humble abode – her bedroom.

Dan found an unusual means of communication, a simple note slipped under the door, seeing as Sarah was disinterested in confronting Dan. She did read the rather long, double-sided note, if only out of curiosity.

> To Dearest Sarah, Dot to Dot Face, Frizzos or Sardines …
> take your pick, you can choose any or all of the above! Hee
> hee xxx
>
> Thanks heaps for reading my letter, it means we are getting
> somewhere in the talking department, as you don't look
> at me for me to apologise or state my case on the events
> surrounding Allyson's party … how could we all forget! Don't
> look so surprised! Leila's brother told me everything you know:
> B-B-RAAAAD, alcohol, Dad slapping you in front of everyone
> … soooo funny I'm cracking up right now.
>
> Okay, don't cry! It'll all be fine once we're in Lebanon, hey?

How exciting, travelling to a place we have only watched on TV. A third world country, 'lucky us' – filled with civil war, lack of water/electricity, poverty and poor infrastructure! Should be their travel slogan!

Want more? I have done a bit of research! Excited yet? I know, I am too! Anyway, Dad wants to marry you off in Lebo Land so desperately, especially after the little stunt you pulled (and you still owe me some cash $$$ so pay up! I followed through with my end of the deal). Dad didn't find out from me, I promise. Again it was Leila's brother, I don't know why he hates his sister so much. Beats me.

Again, I had nothing to do with it, all I heard was the phone ringing PRETTY LATE at 10.45pm when you and Leila were at the party, and I guessed at first it was Leila's mum or dad, but then Dad ran up to me like he was going to kill someone he said 'Who's Tom?' and I figured it had to be Leila's brother! Why was he calling us? What was his motive? Perhaps he didn't have any. Dad didn't say a word to me after that, just started shouting at Mum, then grabbed his keys and I was I left in wonderment and slight panic as to what was going on, although of course I had a hunch what Dad was up to and it wasn't a trip to the local church!

Okay gotta go! In anticipation of a speedy reply … your best bro signing out.

Dan.

Sarah shook as she scattered the pages over her bed and wept quietly. *What the hell did I get myself into?* All she wanted was to grasp the slightest bit of freedom; with this in mind she'd taken 'a leap of faith', one step forward then two steps, back into a harsh reality.

Leila sprung to her mind immediately; Sarah had to call her, but how? Sarah couldn't possibly leave her room to face the unwanted, treacherous music of her parents jabbering. Sarah decided her thirst for knowledge could wait till school the next day.

Sarah knelt down by her bed in a prayer-like position and began uttering the words 'all good things come to me', over and over and began a silent appeal. 'Oh dear Lord, guide me to think positive thoughts and rid me of all the negative energy in my life, help my peers forget all the unfortunate events at Allyson's party. Arise hope, promise and courage in my day-to-day existence. Amen.'

Sarah felt a large weight lift off her shoulders miraculously and breathed easier, knowing some entity was by her side watching over her.

# Chapter Ten

Sarah was late for double period English class to her dismay, as she didn't want to make the grand entrance. Walking into room 109 couldn't have been more of an effort. She entered sweating profusely, attempting not to make eye contact with anyone, although couldn't avoid looking shyly at Spencer, whom was marking class attendance. He always managed to smile at her in a way that her heart sank, skipping a beat. Spencer didn't seem worried upon Sarah's late arrival and appeared happy as usual to see her.

Sarah heard the silent chitter-chatter and sneering giggles and knew for sure it was aimed at her. She took a deep breath and seated herself as usual at the front of the class, the closer the better.

Sarah knew Brad was in class and was seated behind her. As much as she prayed he would ignore her, he kept whispering, 'Sarah, how … how are you to … today?'

As much as Sarah wanted to ignore Brad, she succumbed to his constant pleas and turned around to face him. 'I'm fine Brad! Now can you just chill and let me concentrate on Mr Fitz.'

'Why? Cause you l … le … ike him?'

Sarah made sure her tone was only high enough for Brad to hear her. 'Yes, indeed I do! As only a student could like a teacher.'

It felt like the longest period of English and for the first time, Sarah hated every ticking torturous minute of it (aside from Spencer), as students mocked her asking if she was 'with' Brad now after the party, and if her face still hurt after her dad struck her. It was too much to bear that Sarah was ready to explode and hoped Spencer didn't suspect or hear anything of what was said – but she knew it was all too obvious. Sarah distanced herself from the prodding and poking interrogators and walked towards Spencer, who was reading a black laminate covered book so she couldn't read the title.

'Sir? Um, may I be excused? As I have a massive headache.' Sarah rubbed her brow, trying to hold back the tears.

Spencer looked genuinely concerned. 'Sarah what's wrong, is there anything I can do? You don't look yourself today.'

'Yeah, I'd like to get some fresh air if you don't mind, maybe some Panadol from the nurse's office?' Sarah's voice sounded rather hoarse.

'That's absolutely fine, would you like someone to accompany you?'

As much as she wanted to say, *I want you Spencer*, and felt it was written all over her face, she held back the thought.

Brad raised his hand eagerly. 'I will! I will Mr Fitz ple … please …'

Spencer looked displeased and the entire room became noisy and in disarray. 'Put your hand down, Brad, and continue with your work!'

'Kaaay … gee, I was only tr … trying to he … help.'

Sarah caught Spencer's eye. 'Thanks, Sir, I'll be okay I think.'

Spencer scanned the room and noticed all eyes were on him, quickly regaining composure before raising his voice in a controlled tone, attempting to sound like a sergeant: cold and emotionless. 'Sarah, go to the nurses' office. And make sure you do the rest of your class task at home. There's not much of class left now, so off you go.'

'Thanks Sir, will do.' And with that Sarah was gone, leaving Spencer to eavesdrop on the stream of students' idle chatter circulating Allyson's party.

He did indeed overhear the students raving about Brad kissing Sarah and felt sick to the stomach on revelations about

Sarah's father striking her. He was most displeased to discover Sarah's drunken episode but was not quick to judge her, as his strong feelings outweighed her appropriate behaviour etiquette.

Sarah didn't go to the nurse's office. The bell charmed its way into recess as she looked for Leila. Finally Leila found Sarah on the school oval, Sarah's head lowered as she walked, aimless and detached. Leila felt sorry for her friend and quickly ran up to her, hoping to bring some comfort.

'Oh my God, Leila, I've been hanging out to see you! Tell me out of curiosity, was it your brother? Was it Tom? You know something, I know you do!' Sarah clenched Leila's shirt collar and twisted it repugnantly in anger.

Leila grabbed Sarah's wrists. 'Okay, okay! You can let go now – gee whiz, you are uptight.' Leila adjusted her clothing. 'I really feel for you, I can't begin to fathom what you're going through and if I were you I wouldn't be here today …'

Sarah interrupted. 'Cut the small talk, girl! Tell me what you know!'

'I may have slipped and mentioned something to Tom about your plan,' Leila uttered nervously. 'I'm not one hundred percent sure, yet it had to be him, he didn't admit it but he is worse than Dan. I think they were in on it together!'

Sarah plonked herself down onto the verdant lawn and stretched her legs. Leila sat down beside her and rubbed her back gently.

'Don't stress about it too much Sarah, you and I both know it's inevitable that you are going to Lebanon … as much as I hate the fact, it is what it is!'

'Yeah, perhaps you're right. As much as I hate thinking about it, it has finally hit me and Lebanon is getting closer day by day. If only I had a bit more time with NE. I could never tell him how I feel but he probably knows it already, I make it that obvious!'

'You do; you seem to light up when he's around and you go all bubbly and happy.'

Sarah smiled thinking about Spencer, and then the thought of him quickly became distorted in her mind. 'Did I tell you I locked myself in my room? Well, for a while anyway, trying to escape my parents. Then I had to help my mum with the washing, which I should have tried to flout, and my dad thinks I've got a boyfriend! I'm so sick of their maze of mumbo jumbo.'

Sarah stood up and Leila mirrored her movements. They walked around the oval, talking about Lebanon and the fact that Sarah was going in less than four weeks, sooner than Leila had anticipated. Sarah wished she had Allyson's life; looks and freedom with the advantage of Aussie parents would fulfil her dreams, she thought.

Leila, on the other hand, was more worried about Sarah leaving her, as she was her only true friend and hadn't formed a bond with anyone at school but Sarah. Leila didn't know how she was going to survive her everyday existence without her. 'Don't go for good, Sarah! I still need you. You are my only friend here. I hope you don't forget about me.'

'Never, Leila! How could you say that? Don't worry, we will always keep in touch. As soon as I arrive I'll send you my mailing address and details. Nothing will stand in the way of our friendship. Besides, I don't think my parents could possibly stay in Lebanon for good, simply because their pension money wouldn't be enough to support all of us. I have done a little research, you know, and spoken to our careers teacher. If I have any problems over there I could go to the Australian embassy in Lebanon and they help you if you are in any kind of trouble.'

Leila looked at Sarah long and hard. 'You'll be back soon, I know it! Sooner than we both think and ready for uni. I hope I get into my chosen field, business management! What do you think?'

'I'm sure you'll get in, don't stress too much about it – at least you're not in my predicament! You can enjoy your life in this country while I will be flying over you, wishing I was with you and experiencing what you undergo in this lucky country.'

They both walked to their next class, wishing they had more time together to share their passions – for love they did. If only it could be ever apparent in the eyes of their infatuations, as unrequited love was detrimental to their soul. Only the callous warrior of time would tell.

# Chapter Eleven

Talk of the school formal soon circulated and became the central theme of conversation. This particular event sparked Sarah's interest, especially as it was going to be held precisely one week before her dreaded departure to Lebanon. Sarah wasn't sure if she would be able to go at first. But on discussing it with her parents, she told them that it was compulsory and every student had to go or the principle would ask to speak to them to arrange a meeting. Marrouf and Jamal didn't want to seem unreasonable and agreed to let Sarah go to the formal, on the grounds it was the last school event and they would have complete control over her in Lebanon.

Sarah was over the moon, flight plans aside – she was so excited she couldn't wait to tell Leila the good news. It was the last night she would spend with Spencer and she hoped something would happen between them or at least expose their feelings; even if there was an inkling of doubt, Sarah longed for some kind of revelation.

Sarah spoke on the phone to Leila later that night, both in high spirits as the thought of seeing and perhaps having one single dance with their boys was too much to absorb for one night. They shared latest dress fashion choices, hairstyles and trends, even exchanging *Cosmopolitan* and *Dolly* makeup and dress tips. This proved highly useful in their pursuit to looking and feeling a million dollars (or at least, that's how it read in the magazine). Sarah's happy thoughts soon acquired a sour angle and Dan was on her mind in a destructive way as she wondered if he would plot to ruin her again during a crucial event in her life. Sarah decided, as she was not on communicative terms with Dan, that she would write a reply to his letter – or more so a threat on his life if he was to hinder her freedom again.

To Dearest Dan, my one and only bro! I guess your letter had some impact on me, cause here I am writing you a heartfelt reply to your charming letter of apology ... or confession?

I must add before you begin to challenge your brain, I know it was you and Tom that planned to ruin me. Don't even think to deny it! I should have known better not to trust you and I don't owe you a cent!

In fact you owe me big time! You will only ever be my brother biologically and not my ally. How naive was I to think we could form a partnership, looking out for one another. I will never forgive you for this.

For all the turmoil you put me through, you've made Mum and Dad doubt and mistrust me and now I'm the laughing stock at school. So much for working my way up the popularity ladder! You have taken everything I have strived for, most of all my pride. So my loving brother, in terms of Lebanon I know everything, from the beggars on the streets, to downtown high life in central Beirut, where all the tourists enjoy fine wine and dining. See, I have done my research too! How could my life get any worse than it already is? So, I pledge to make yours a living hell!

Payback time, I say! Watch your back, Dandino, and if anything goes wrong in my life again, I won't ask any questions. You will suffer in slow and painful torturous vengeance – I have an appetite for it!

Many thanks,

Sarah.

Sarah slid her note under Dan's door, feeling an overwhelming satisfaction as she had put all she needed to express to Dan on paper. Sarah had mixed feelings – excitement in relation to the formal dance, and stress with plans of Lebanon – but she held her head high, never showing her parents what a wreck she was internally.

The next morning at school, there was talk of the last school dance and girls were raving about what places to shop for their outfits. Sarah knew it was not her place to ask her parents to pay for a dress. She was presently not in their good books – if they had any books left for her, except the one titled 'marriage' detailing how quickly they had to marry her off before she found some no-good 'Aussie' boy.

Sarah secretly kept money in a book that she had saved over the years; she would place each single note neatly within the pages of her thick science fiction novel, which Sarah believed brought her luck and good fortune. Sarah thought she wouldn't tell her parents and buy the dress herself with her own money, as there was already nervous tension between them.

The next obstacle was how she was going to go shopping without her parents' knowledge. Then she figured she would say she borrowed the dress from Leila and skip a couple of classes to shop, hoping her coffin wouldn't be lowered further into the deep cavity of self-destruction.

Double period of English was the last lesson for the day. Sarah was pleased, as she couldn't think of anything better than to end the day staring at Spencer as he discussed the tasks ahead, even though she paid little attention. Instead she pondered them in the future being alone and happy together, smiling, laughing and reminiscing on old times.

Spencer would look at her almost too often, even going to the extent of sitting on a desk directly in front of her; if body language could talk, Spencer would have made his feelings towards her too obvious. Sarah would give him her utmost attention, constantly making mischievous eye contact (luckily without students' prying eyes). She did indeed enchant him with her charisma and he felt drawn into her like a giant wave crashing onto the shoreline.

A student asked at random, 'So, Sir! Are you going to the formal?'

'Yes, I think I will as all the year twelve teachers are invited,' said Spencer as he adjusted his tie and Sarah sighed with relief.

'What are you going to wear, Mr Fitz?' somebody yelled across the room.

'I'm sure I'll figure something out! Have you?' Spencer pounced. He clapped his hands. 'Okay now, settle down class, back to work, you know you have exams before the formal, so concentrate on your study habits – your futures are at stake.'

There was a thunderous moan across the room as students were brought back to the stressful realities of school exams.

Sarah thought about Lebanon and exams were the last thing on her mind. How could she erase these pent-up feelings and the resentment towards her parents – and Dan, for that matter? She turned and looked at Spencer only for one tenth of a second and felt a warmth within her no words could express, and all negative energy drained through a crack in the old stained classroom window.

# Chapter Twelve

Exams had commenced and concluded so quickly Sarah felt she didn't even have time to scratch her head or pluck an eyebrow. She hadn't pampered herself, as she was too absorbed in her books and memorised loads of information. Mentally and physically she was drained, and lack of sleep didn't help either. She was at her wits' end juggling so many balls between exams, Lebanon, her parents and Leila. Unfortunately Spencer was not part of the mix, although he kept her afloat. In an insane world, the thought of Spencer was her sanity.

Sarah was pleased with her Literature exam and knew she did extremely well. The exam was held in the school library and Sarah suspected Spencer was close by, as she felt his presence gave her inspiration; no other exam had been like this one. She wished he were at every assessment task. Her suspicions were right: as she left the room, he was there waiting with an alluring smile. Sarah didn't care that Chris Ricardo, the most popular guy at school, was trying to strike conversation and appeared interested in her. Nothing else mattered to her anymore – not that of popularity, or the good-looking heartthrobs her school had on display.

All that inspired and drove Sarah through her final year of school was the man whom she'd grown to love.

Her parents didn't hassle her about her exams, not even asking her how she went in her examinations. Sarah was relieved that they didn't pay much attention to her, as they were too self-absorbed arranging travel plans, suitcases, presents and pension payments.

Dan and Sarah never spoke to each other, especially after Sarah's letter, only exchanging unpleasant glances at one another from time to time. She wasn't sure if Dan even read her letter, but felt she had to give him the silent treatment for her own pride and dignity.

The school formal struck so suddenly, like a sharp slap in the face – unlike the fierce lash from her father, Sarah welcomed the event with favourable nervousness. Fortunately enough, Marrouf and Jamal didn't ask any questions when Sarah mentioned Leila's mum was picking her up to get dressed and ready for their big night at their house.

Leila was delighted to see Sarah and discover they both purchased black dresses. Sarah wasn't fazed by this and figured most girls would be wearing black anyway, as a 'little black dress' was so versatile and timeless.

'At long last, Sarah! Tonight's the night we either land flat on our faces and crash and burn, or have the time of our lives and our crushes finally tell us they feel the same way we do about them.'

Sarah frowned as she pulled out her makeup bag and began applying lipstick. 'As long as it's nothing like Allyson's party, setting off a domino effect of ruthless mishaps.'

'Yeah, as long as you don't drink or go anywhere near Brad, you'll be fine.'

'Gee, thanks for the encouragement! I don't think there'll be an open bar or anything and I certainly have learnt my lesson.'

Leila began straightening her hair. 'Sarah, can you help me with the back of my hair? It's always harder to straighten the back!'

'Yeah, sure, babe, that's why I'm here.'

Both girls put on their dresses, heels and accessories. It was almost 6 pm and the night was still young.

Sarah and Leila both looked at one another in the mirror and smiled cheerfully. They were both happy with the way they looked, as weeks and weeks of preparation proved quite rewarding.

Most students hired limousines or carpooled. Leila's dad, however, was more than happy to drive the pair and made a quick exit so no one saw them. As they entered the venue, Sarah's lace rose-pattern chiffon black dress attracted admiring eyes and expressions of how beautiful she looked. Leila was out of the picture for a while. Sarah scanned the room but there was no sign of Spencer anywhere.

Later, she noticed some teachers were sitting on the one table; along with them, Sarah spotted Spencer looking ever so handsome in a pastel grey coloured suit, white shirt and a blue tie, which Sarah felt was a good choice as it brought out his striking blue eyes. She also wondered why Spencer sat with the younger cooler teachers and not his mentors.

Leila nudged Sarah. 'Did you see how hot CA looks in his suit? So sharp and look at those arms, looks like those bulges are going to pop out of that tux, I tell ya.'

Sarah's eyes were still on Spencer. 'Yeah, he looks quite impressive.' Sarah's mind was not with Leila. Suddenly a dark shadow blocked her view of Spencer.

'Sah … Sarah! You l … look am … a … zing.' Brad stammered and looked at Sarah with immense intensity.

'Oh, that's so sweet. Thanks, Brad, you brush up pretty good yourself.'

Leila pulled Sarah's arm. 'Thanks Brad, nice bow tie!' said Leila mockingly as she dragged Leila to CA's table.

'Sorry girls!' Allyson said with a grim laugh. 'This table is taken if you hadn't noticed.'

Leila rolled her eyes and whispered to Sarah, 'Oh my god, did you see what that bitch was wearing! What's with that look, hot pants and a boob tube! Screams "take me baby, I'm easy." I wish CA had better taste!'

Sarah sighed and said, 'Well if he did, he'd be with you.'

Leila smiled warmly at Sarah. 'I wish,' Leila replied. They finally found their table. It may as well have been named the 'brain table' as those whom were seated were house captains and the student representative council. Sarah was thrilled; she felt privileged to be seated alongside the intellectuals of the school, hoping Spencer was aware of this.

She held the menu close and chose the veal marsala with wild mushrooms for her main course. Sarah's appetite was in fine form this evening, especially as she was happy. The music was felt throughout the room and the cool beats and thumps drew Sarah onto the dance floor, where she sang and danced to 'Boom Boom Shake the Room'.

Leila danced alongside her and Sarah scanned the room for Spencer. He was still seated, signing yearbooks; she wondered if he would eventually make it to the dance floor.

Leila pinched Sarah. 'Ouch, what was that for?' cried Sarah.

'Look! Allyson and CA making out!'

Sarah cringed. 'Gross! I didn't want to see that, thanks Leila.'

Sarah needed a drink and made her way back to her table, where she poured herself a glass of water, asking herself, 'Is my glass half full or half empty?' *Definitely half full*, she thought, as she felt positive and in full spirits. Sarah looked over at Spencer and she knew he didn't see her gaze; she longed to run towards him and ask him for a slow dance. Sarah turned and headed towards the dance floor to find Leila. She didn't know how Spencer got in front of her so quickly – as she recalled he was seated.

Spencer uttered ever so swiftly and quietly, 'Sarah, make sure you save a dance for me, okay?'

Sarah didn't answer, she knew her smile gleamed from her inner being, internally igniting a twinkle in her eyes.

She danced all night, hardly returning to her table. Even when Spencer danced close to her, she couldn't strike up the courage to approach him and he didn't make any attempt to sway her.

Photographers snapped shots of students on the dance floor and group snaps of them seated. Awards and credits to teachers were acknowledged. Sarah longed to be one of those students who presented Spencer a bottle of wine (and maybe a quick peck on the cheek), but 'Handsome Daniel' was given the opportunity and Spencer looked pleased with this as her stomach sunk into a poisoning whirlpool of jealousy.

The school formal ended with empty doubt and dissuasion; Sarah's dance of a lifetime with Spencer had not arisen, though the opportunity was ever present. Saddened by how the night had unfolded into nothingness, Sarah walked over to the display table where all the graduates' photos for the night were on show for all to see and purchase. She didn't come across her individual photo and figured someone must have bought it – but whom?

Sarah turned to her friend with a look that she assumed Leila understood. Leila looked puzzled and wavered her head from side to side. 'Don't look at me, I didn't buy your photo, are you kidding me?'

'Okay, if you didn't, who did?'

Leila shrugged, 'Maybe NE! He was checking you out, like, all night.'

'Well, if he did, I feel flattered, but not as impressed as if he asked me to dance … anyway, shit happens. Hopefully fate will find another day or way to bring us together.'

Sarah and Leila slowly walked out through the formal doors, leaving behind their dreams, passions and yearning desires. They were defeated once again by the obstacles destiny thrusts out to waiver and dampen your stride.

Inner voices of strength echoed in Sarah's head, keeping her afloat in shivery shark-infested waters embedding doubt.

# Chapter Thirteen

Sarah held her head high, even though she felt immense stabbing pains in her throat and stomach. Marrouf and Jamal purchased their suitcases from the local op shop and Sarah began to fold her clothes tidily into what looked and smelt like a vintage Depression-era suitcase. *Amazing what you can find at a second hand shop*, Sarah mused.

Jamal forced her way as usual into Sarah's bedroom, not bothering to knock or be courteous, as she felt there was no need for Sarah to have privacy. 'Sarah! You like your suitcase? Only \$20 for four suitcases, beautiful! Your father good haggler, eh?' Jamal waved the items of clothing in her hands. 'And just look, I bought you a few blouses; they look as good as new. I wash, *habibti*, then you try on!'

Sarah nodded and mumbled under her breath. She couldn't believe how cheap her parents were and felt rather embarrassed; if only she was strong enough and had more money, what it would be like to live alone and be free of her parents? Freedom seemed so out of reach, while fear and self-doubt hindered her pursuit for happiness.

Sarah knew too well she only had one single week in Melbourne, before she would be boarding a plane to reach a world she had no desire to inhabit.

Spencer would always linger in the back of her mind, no matter what life dished out. He was there and remained in her subconscious. Sarah thought it useless to think anything could happen between them; even if it did, she didn't think she was good enough for him or on his level, as he was so well accomplished. Spencer had a career, a car, money, intelligence and pride. Sarah believed she had none of the above and this, as well as her leaving soon, depressed her immensely.

***

The days grew rapid as nights became long and wretched, she couldn't get any shuteye tossing and turning in her bed. Sarah was miserable and it showed as she neglected herself and Jamal's cooking (to Dan's delight).

Before Sarah could say her goodbyes, the day had come sooner than expected. She gazed out of her passenger window at the Departure sign as they arrived at the Melbourne airport. Sarah had no time to see Leila or wish her farewell as she made sure her parents dotted their I's and crossed their T's with passports and paperwork surrounding their flight plans. Sarah's uncle Amo Farrouk was kind enough to drive the family to the airport and assist his brother Marrouf with collecting mail and house maintenance issues, also making sure Marrouf and Jamal's pension money was transferred directly to Lebanon.

Sarah had butterflies in her belly and wasn't feeling too well; Dan didn't help the situation as he smirked and sang aloud mockingly. 'Sarah, sweet Dot to Dot Face, she's so excited to go to Lebo Land and find the man of her dreams. She will accept any man, age no exception, as long as he is Druze … la la laah …' Dan opened his arms wide like a dancer at the end of a stage act.

Sarah tugged at her mother's cardigan. 'Mum! Could you shut Dan's ugly mouth before I left hook him and send him plummeting on his backside!'

'Dandino! Sarah! Enough, *yih*! You both acting like little kids. Sarah, help your dad fill out the flight cards for the family.'

'Sure, Mum, anything's better than listening to Dan's ugly voice.'

Sarah's parents bid farewell to Amo Farrouk. He was the only relative at the airport, which wasn't unusual as her parents didn't interact with many people, nor did they have many friends. Sarah waited in the queue with her family, dragging her suitcase behind her and dodging eye contact with Dan, who had a grin from ear to ear. Sarah kept busy completing the flight cards, even one for Dan; it crossed her mind to tamper with his information but felt she was way over her head with her parents already.

Their luggage was finally weighed and Sarah felt uncomfortable while Marrouf hurled rude and presumptuous comments at the airlines officer in charge, as he couldn't afford extra luggage fees.

As Sarah inhaled all her unwanted anxieties, she exuded relief, believing she had to face her fears headstrong if she was going to make it through this journey. Sarah felt if she did conquer the unknown, if she liked it or not, she'd come out of this a stronger and more independent woman. She had never even travelled interstate or investigated the undeniable beauty that Melbourne or its outskirts had to offer.

At the flight check-in, the rather attractive and flawless airline attendant smiled warmly. 'Welcome to Qantas Airways, enjoy your flight.' This woman ripped the tickets and they finally boarded the plane.

'Travel broadens the mind,' said Dan dryly.

Sarah uttered with self-assurance, 'You can take the man out of the country, but you can't take the country out of the man.'

Dan clapped his hands, quite amused and not fazed by curious on-looking passengers. 'Bravo, bravo child! I mean Sarah … sis.' Dan grinned.

Sarah couldn't resist and smiled faintly. Marrouf and Jamal were seated directly in front of the pair. Dan hastily acquired the window seat. Marrouf turned, looked over his uncomfortable economy class seat and adjusted it to his liking, even though Sarah felt compressed like in a pickle jar.

Marrouf looked at Sarah. 'You know *habibti*, sixteen hours and four minutes approximately and we land on our home soil, Beirut Airport!'

'Yippee!' bellowed Dan excitedly, only to annoy Sarah.

'You know, Dandino, you are going to love Lebanon and wish we had come sooner. You, too, Sarah, you gonna say, "Mum, we never want to come back to Azzie-tralia."'

Before Sarah could utter a word in disapproval, knowing those last four minutes were going to literally kill her, the airline hostess approached, stating to observe and follow the seatbelt green light alert.

Sarah closed her eyes, relaxed her muscles and thought about Spencer, his smile and charming gaze when his eyes met hers. Was he thinking about her too? Then, like a forceful wave over sand those sweet thoughts were soon swept away by Dan's annoying beatboxing. Sarah did in fact bring an escape in the form of a Charles Dickens novel, *Great Expectations*. She flicked through it to find her bookmark and resumed her journey.

When Sarah wasn't reading or eating what tasted like bland hospital food, she dozed in and out of sleep, hoping this was all a bad dream. She hoped this was a mere manifestation of insanity and that she'd wake up in the comfort of her own room in familiar surroundings.

Hours passed. Sarah felt she had to stretch her legs, so she stood and walked down the narrow aisle towards the toilet to freshen up. She noticed many of the passengers were Middle Eastern in appearance and wondered if they were all travelling to Lebanon, as there were a few stops before they reached their destination at Rafic Hariri International Airport. Their first stop from Melbourne was Kuala Lumpur Airport, followed by Dubai.

As Sarah entered the cubicle she found it small and restricting and felt a bit queasy with the unexpected clear air turbulence. Sarah touched her face as she looked in the mirror and thought it didn't do her justice, or the lighting was all wrong, as her blemishes and pimples looked so defined and inflamed. Sarah thought she must be dehydrated and that was the reason her skin looked utterly blemished.

Returning to her seat, she found Dan asleep and took the opportunity to look out the window, observing the aircraft wing and the astronomical height they had reached. Melbourne seemed so out of reach even in her memories. 'Out of sight, out of mind' didn't ring true when she pondered Spencer.

# Chapter Fourteen

## *Arrival in Lebanon*

The final destination at Beirut Airport, Lebanon hit Sarah like a ton of bricks and quickly became a reality. 'This is it!' she said to herself as she adjusted her clothing and reached for her hand luggage situated above her seat. Sarah believed this moment in time was destined from the day she was born into this world; being raised by Arabic parents, it was inevitable they would want to revisit their hometown one day.

The words 'welcome to Lebanon' rang in her ears as Sarah stepped off the aircraft and boarded the airport bus that would take all passengers to the airport entrance. Marrouf instantly greeted a handsome man in uniform, shaking his hand with a customary greeting kiss on either side of his face. Marrouf introduced Sarah to this young man named Tarek as a cousin on her mother's side of the family. Sarah found him charming, especially wearing the Arab police uniform that was a lovely royal blue and white military camouflage pattern. She found him to be quite good looking and mysterious with dark eyes, shaven military hair and of medium height.

'*Ahlan*,' said Tarek, looking directly at Sarah and pulled out his hand.

Sarah shook it. 'Hello, pleased to meet you!' she said, trying to avoid speaking Arabic. Sarah could speak Lebanese fluently, but she'd never learned to write it.

Marrouf interjected before the pair could exchange words and began to ask him a series of questions about his parents, where they were living and life in Lebanon. From what Sarah gathered from their conversation, Tarek was happy in Lebanon, residing in Beirut and enjoying his job being highly respected in the community. Sarah felt the weight of Tarek's eyes on her, which made her feel uncomfortable. She turned in her seat, trying to pretend she wasn't eavesdropping by looking out of the bus window and making useless conversation with her mother, but Jamal was engaging in the chinwag between Marrouf and Tarek as well.

Sarah felt the bus come to a halt, and felt a little at ease now that they had finally reached the entrance of Rafic Hariri International Airport. Tarek expressed to Marrouf that the family come visit for lunch one day and Marrouf nodded approval with the word *enshallah* (God willing). Sarah didn't look at Tarek to say goodbye as they got off at the bus terminal. She felt shy and didn't want him to think she was interested – although strangely enough, he did remind her of Spencer.

Dan nudged Sarah to get her attention in order to look at homeless people or beggars sitting on the entrance floor at the airport. This particular lady caught Sarah's eye, as her face looked drained and the black around her eyes prominent. She seemed tired and worn out, with a grubby mustard cloth covering her entire body; a baby lay stretched on her thighs, her hand in a cup-like position. Sarah found this picture quite disturbing; never in her life had she seen something so unnerving. She looked to her father as pity embraced her to ask for some money to give these people, but Marrouf had problems of his own, dealing with men fighting over their suitcases as they fought and fussed over Sarah and her family like drunken pirates discovering hidden treasure – as all tourists were greeted in this way.

Marrouf accepted the offer of one of the desperate strangers to drive them to their destination, but not without payment.

Once Marrouf handed him some cash, the man was pleased and at the family's disposal. Marrouf explained they were headed to his brother's house in country village Btâtar, situated near the cities of Bhamdoun and Aley. Sarah was feeling anxious and excited at the same time; she felt that she could learn to come to terms with this country, as they were indeed treated like royalty, unlike how they were living back home in an undesirable and poor neighbourhood.

Sarah thought that there would be chaos and mayhem and army troops filling the streets, as conveyed on the news, but quite the contrary. Lebanon seemed a panorama of unique splendour, peaceful and liveable.

Btâtar, the place where Marrouf grew up, had beauty and tranquillity with its country feel, a land of great natural charm and one crammed with antiquities of immense interest, mountains and open savannah. Wonderful blossoming grapevines were popular, with fruit-filled trees as well as olive trees. The roads, however, were rocky and infrastructure was poor. As a constant topic of conversation Marrouf would often say thanks to the government rewarding their own pockets instead of sustaining and maintaining the general standard of living.

Sarah felt he was indeed omniscient – as in his name, meaning 'to know' – which lead her to tread ever so carefully she felt he knew what was on her mind.

Jamal sighed relief when they had arrived at their destination in front of Marrouf's house, where he had grown up with his six brothers and three sisters, one of whom passed away when she was three months old. Sarah asked Marrouf how his younger sibling died and he explained he was only four years old when she passed away; he remembered his mum saying they found her body frozen solid without a pulse left outside in the cold, deserted by her older sister after being given a bath. This story still remained a mystery and Sarah didn't want to delve too deeply into the nitty-gritties of it, feeling sorry for the older sister having to live with the guilt and blame for such a tragedy.

The driver helped Marrouf unload the suitcases from the ramshackle station wagon and Sarah couldn't help but notice the expression on her father's face as he stopped dead in his tracks. His jaw dropped, which turned into a loving warm smile. A man appeared through the doorway, followed by a woman and their three children. '*Hamdellah allah salama.*' (Praise be to God. You're home safe.)

Marrouf dropped his suitcase and marched speedily and open-armed towards his brother, embracing him firmly. Sarah had never seen Marrouf so responsive. 'Essam, my younger brother! It's been so long.'

'Too long!' said Essam as he touched his belly and remarked how Marrouf had put on weight. Marrouf expressed amusement and breathed in all he could of his childhood memories and surrounding Lebanese atmosphere.

Sarah noticed Marrouf's eyes welling up with tears and for once in her life, she felt she understood the meaning of family and culture and the fundamental reasons they were here.

She greeted her cousins. Jamal had shown her photos of them in an album at home, so Sarah felt she knew them. Nabila was the eldest child in the family and the same age as Sarah, followed by her younger brother Nadir, whom was double Sarah's height and youngest sister Arish. Aunty Haifa was extremely hospitable and was quick to gather a wonderful meal fit for a king. Aunty Haifa mentioned that you always had to have olives on your table with your meal as it was called '*sheikh al-sofra*' (head of the table).

Dan announced without hesitation, 'Is that why there are so many olive trees here?'

Haifa laughed and squeezed Dan's cheeks. Sarah thought if only her aunt squeezed a little harder, she would have felt quite satisfied. Jamal commented how beautiful and grown up the children were to Essam and he stated, 'My girls will help me with my old age, but my boy will bring the death of me.'

Everybody laughed, especially Sarah; she thought her father should adopt that very notion. Instead Marrouf frowned at Sarah – she knew too well what he was thinking and it didn't correspond with his brother's theory.

Sarah helped Jamal and Haifa clear the table while the men lit cigarettes and went for a leisurely stroll outside. Nabila and Arish expressed their happiness to see Sarah and her family, and she was equally pleased to meet them as well. 'So Nabila, are you in year twelve now?'

'Yes, my last year, then university.'

Sarah looked pleased. 'Oh, that's great Nabila! What kind of work do you want to do?'

'I would love to be a teacher, how about yourself?'

'Teaching sounds good, although if I was smart enough I'd love to have a law degree under my sleeve! But I want to see if I can get into AUB first as I have completed year twelve and Dad said that's the best uni in Lebanon.'

'Yes, it is very expensive! But tomorrow my dad will take you to see if your year twelve certificate will get you in to uni … you might have to do year twelve again before you can be accepted, as our education standards are much higher than yours in Australia.'

Sarah looked like she'd seen a ghost. 'Oh, I didn't know that – now you've got me worried.' Sarah wasn't happy and was dubious having to repeat year twelve again, as it was so hard and stressful the first time around – to do it all again and in another country was distressing to say the least.

# Chapter Fifteen

Days rapidly flew by, dramatically turning into weeks. Sarah had settled in quite well and became accustomed to traditional gatherings at her uncle's home, which was a central meeting place for relatives and unexpected guests – or future prospects for 'husband material' as Jamal would often whisper in Sarah's ear.

Sarah didn't like it one little bit that young men, middle-aged and even old gentlemen would ask for her hand in marriage. This way of courting confused Sarah, as she felt everything in the way of relationships was done in reverse – the male proposes marriage if you agree on terms of initial attraction then you are to be engaged, and that's your chance to get to know them like a boyfriend/girlfriend with the promise you will be married.

Nabila was very well educated and articulate. Her Arabic accent was prominent when speaking English. Although Nabila was chubby (or for want of a better word, 'big boned'), Sarah thought her to be quite attractive, having a round face with soft white pale skin, her facial bones gleaming through a beautiful smile. There was a grace about her.

Nabila would often joke that because she didn't have a visa and wasn't born in Australia she wouldn't get as many proposals for marriage as Sarah, and pleaded with her that if she ever returned to Australia, she'd sponsor Nabila to come for a holiday. Sarah laughed and as much as she knew Nabila meant well, she was completely and utterly right: it was the visa all these men wanted. She couldn't fathom why there was so much interest in Australia if they hadn't even been there.

Nabila said mockingly, 'Oh Sarah, they must think they can pick money off the trees in Australia!'

'Yeah, there are so many trees in Australia, mostly deciduous so they wouldn't have to pick them as they would fall at their feet.'

Nabila looked puzzled. 'Did you say ridiculous?'

'No! *Deciduous*, meaning shedding of leaves, falling off at maturity.'

Nabila headed for the kitchen and asked Sarah if she'd like some maté tea. Sarah told her she had to go to her room and would join her shortly. She was indeed homesick, seeking comfort in books and journal writing.

## FIRST JOURNAL ENTRY IN LEBANON

'It's often just enough to be with someone. I don't need to
touch them. Not even talk. A feeling passes between you both.
YOU'RE NOT ALONE.' – Marilyn Monroe.

A few weeks have passed and I'm here in Lebanon, the place I
now call home, the place I dreaded to come. Now I'm here and
it was destined, written in the old ancient books, in the stars
and meant to be. University, to Dad's convenience, is swept
well under the carpet, it saddens me to write.

My first encounter with a strange man, what my lovely
mother called marriage material: from the moment I saw him,
I wasn't the slightest bit impressed, nor was he of I. This man
was double my height with a plain face and an incorrectly
aligned nose. He didn't even smile when he greeted me! First
impressions are always the best, so he ticked all the wrong
boxes. He mainly spoke with Mum and Dad, barely even
looking at me or directing any of the conversation my way. I

felt like shouting out, 'Hello, I'm here! If you want to attract my attention you're definitely travelling down the wrong path! As lovely Grandma would say, "There are three things that make a great relationship: attraction, trust and respect. If you have all three, you will live a wonderful life with your partner, but it has to work both ways!"'

Subsequently, another time this guy looked around my age, accompanying his mum. Very charming and looked like handsome Daniel from school, but his mum did all the talking and that was that! Never saw him again. Mum said he wasn't coming to propose – besides, he is Muslim and we are Druze!

Then there was Tarek: 'Army Boy', I call him. I guess I have a weakness for him because he was the first guy I saw in Lebanon and he reminded me somewhat of Spencer. I guess no one could compare to the love of my life!

Nabila found Tarek attractive as well and mentioned that he fancied his cousin and that they've had an ongoing relationship for a while. I guess that was vindicated when he came over to Uncle Essam's place, his arm bracing hers. Although charming, I could not escape the true chemistry between him and his cousin. He even mentioned that he could never get married as there were too many pretty girls and he wouldn't know how to choose, but I knew where his heart was. Perhaps it was a good thing we shared in common the fact that our hearts were in different places and it felt like we understood one another … Tarek and I, even though the attraction was ever evident, would be happy to remain only cousins.

Nabila entered the room as Sarah dropped her pen and covered her journal with an item of clothing that was resting on the bed. Sarah liked to keep her journal private, like her hidden secret of expression.

Nabila and Sarah chatted for hours on end, forming their growing union. The two were from diverse worlds and astronomical light years away – well, that's how it felt to Sarah but they shared a connection with combined equal beliefs and love of life.

Lebanon! Sarah was finally here and excited with what lay ahead. She was willing to take everything that life had to dish out on her. Sarah didn't want to overwrite the fact that she could find true love even if she knew Spencer was the one for her, the kindred spirit, the profound inner deep connection that was bound to her like an attachment imprinted into her soft, pale skin.

# Chapter Sixteen

Lebanon! With its Druze people having struggled for hundreds of years residing in the mountains, existing in a very fractious part of the world under Israeli, Lebanese and Syrian jurisdiction. Druze reputation stand proud and spirited, families and villages left alone by different empires that have passed through because of their rich uniqueness and supporters of each other. Sarah found it to be abundant with culture and custom, being a tightly knit religious community in that everything you did – even, as a manner of speaking, going to the toilet – did not feel like your own personal ritual.

Sarah at times felt like the lowest common denominator, not really knowing what to do with herself, feeling strange and unaccomplished. Sarah didn't have any real goals at this time – only to get up in the morning, dress and go with no real destination in mind. She seldom thought about Spencer to her own amazement, focusing her energies on reading and planning to get some kind of job to get her mind off things.

Sarah found the community of Btâtar to consist of country folk being raised in or living in a rural environment, old fashioned in their ways. Sarah overheard her uncle Essam and father talking about bombings in Tyre (Sour), which juts out from the coast of the Mediterranean about 83 km south of Beirut. Tyre is the fourth largest city of Lebanon. Sarah knew of bombings in Beirut and surrounding areas but never imagined them to be so close, almost next door so to speak. She only heard of such things on the news but never thought for one second it would become reality for her. Sarah, although aware of such civil devastation and chaos, was not frightened, as her uncle Essam and fellow Lebanese citizens reassured her that they were not in danger and had ample knowledge and caution in safe travel routes if needed.

Marrouf while drinking his traditional Arab coffee, looked at Sarah and exclaimed, '*Habibti*, call your mother and Dan, we are going to visit the holy sites. There are many sacred holy sites for the Druze like Sayyid Abdullah, Nabi Ayyub, Set Shaeweni and el-Maqam el-Sharif in Shamlikh to name only a few. It will be good for you to visit these religious temples to bring you closer with our Druze faith.'

'Yes, Dad, thanks, sounds good – I'll go see where Mum is now.'

And with all plans in place, Uncle Essam and family headed to Nabi Ayyub, the holy temple where all Druze have at one time or another prayed and touched their rich, sacred history. The temples are the most important worship places for the Druze; Sarah found these sites enriching, strengthening her spirit and yearning desire to be brought closer to God.

The drive to Shamlikh was picturesque. Sarah thought Lebanon was indeed a beautiful country. Jamal described it well, as it was just as she imagined – with the exception of some of the people who weren't peacemakers and had succumbed to war, chaos, looting and violence.

Sarah felt a sense of ardour that consumed her when they reached the location in Sharon Town, in Shamlikh district, Aley Province. Nabila motioned to Sarah to take off her shoes before entering the holy shrine and handed her a white veil to cover her head as a form of respect. As soon as Sarah entered the blessed chamber, sheer jubilation engulfed her and she felt at peace for the first time upon arrival in Lebanon. She looked around in wonderment, thinking about the Druze identity and its long history of religious secrecy, and the human connection to God.

Nabila uttered quietly while kneeling on a sacred plaque what Sarah interpreted, 'Quench our yearning thirst with goodwill and reflection ... only a few droplets of a colossal ocean of knowledge.' Sarah prayed to God to give her strength and willpower. Her thoughts circled Leila and how she must stay in contact with her best friend; she made a pact with herself on such holy grounds that she would write her a letter.

In the midst of her deep thoughts she looked up at Dan, whom thought this all too amusing – his devious smirk said it all. He looked like he was taking this vacation in his stride and didn't look fazed in the slightest. Sarah felt terribly jealous of her brother taking himself lightly, not having to worry about an arranged marriage or love interest that he left behind in Australia. Dan had started college and formed friendships all in such a short time – contrary to Sarah, who spent her days wallowing in her own self-pity.

The trip home was a rocky one, such that Uncle Essam joked how if they had eaten, even a baby unwelcomed the need to be burped. They all laughed and were pleasantly in high spirits after the outing; even Sarah felt a sense of elation and unearthed an inner peace. Sarah wondered about their Druze religion and confessed to Nabila she would love to find out more about her religion, the secrecy and so-called 'Book of Wisdom'. 'Nabila, do you know where Druze originated from, like the history? It's all so fascinating, our secretive religious community that is closed to outsiders. Tell me what you know, everything.'

'Sure Sarah, what would you like to know? What the Druze means? Who we are?' Nabila replied.

Sarah nodded and winked at Nabila. 'Yes, precisely, please do tell.'

'Okay, well, firstly I read somewhere that the Druze religion was established in Cairo in 1017. Al-Hakim was the Egyptian ruler who founded the Druze religion in the early eleventh century. We are a branch of Islam, containing elements of Christianity, Judaism and Islam. Funnily enough, you won't believe this, but you know the calf?'

'Yeah, those cute baby cows?' Sarah said light-heartedly.

'Some people think that the calf, so to speak, represents the demon in the Druze religion and is a vital symbol which represents the negative forces in the world.'

'No way, but those cute animals that become cows and provide milk, cheese and meat to human beings?'

'Precisely, and it's funny to think and rather contradictory as Al-Hakim blended Islam's belief in one god with Greek thought and Hindu influences.'

Sarah intercepted. 'Hindu influences? But Hindus honour and adore the cow and believe that it is a symbol of the Earth, the nourisher. The cow is so generous, taking nothing but water, grass and grain. There's a lot that remains a mystery with Druze none of us can argue because we don't really know and remain oblivious to the truth, as we don't hold the key! *Kitab al-Hikma*'.

'True, you can't always believe what you read, I'll have to do some of my own research to uncover the truth … so what else … tell me about transmigration of souls? That I find particularly intriguing.'

Nabila resumed. 'The Druze believe that after death, people come back to earth in another body. The dead are given a new life. They believe that the quality of a person's life determines the quality of his/her future lives. A moral person is to be rewarded with a virtuous life again. Druze believe the opposite holds true for those who live an evil life, kinda like karma.'

'Nabila, you know so much – I guess as you were born and raised, live and breathe our religion.' Sarah sighed. 'Is there any way you could get your hands on the so-called Book of Wisdom?'

'No way, Sarah! Besides, you don't know how to read Arabic and I'm not prepared to translate, as … oh, that would be excruciating and painfully long, like interpreting a Shakespearian sonnet.'

Sarah merely shrugged. 'Okay, okay I'll find a way without you – where there's a will, there's a Book of Wisdom.'

Upon arrival at Uncle Essam's house, Nabila walked away and tried to brush off what Sarah said with humour and the fact she had to help her mother with preparation for lunch.

With all the talk of religion prying on Sarah's mind, she soon transposed her thoughts in a secure segment in her mind and focused on getting her letter written and posted to Leila. She made herself comfortable on the rustic oak wood desk in Nabila's room, accompanied by a comfy adjustable chair and she altered it to her liking. Sarah grasped her favourite pen and journal and began.

To Dearest Leila,

How are you? My best friend, to tell you the truth, I miss the hell out of you! Words can't express the hollowness inside my heart, but finally I found the time to compile a letter for you.

Lebanon! Well, hell yeah! I'm here and raring to go … well, that's the attitude I must retain, if I'm ever going to keep my sanity. And don't worry, I'm not married yet (go figure), although I'm sure my loving parents will think of some ingenious plight to get me hitched.

I'm keeping my wits about me. Well, you're probably wondering if I still think about Mr Fitz and I will answer that question by redirecting it your way and ask you how you feel about CA … and there's your answer. What a stupid question indeed! Bloody hell Leila, now you got me started.

I miss him so much that it feels like missing a piece in my jigsaw puzzle that took years to construct! If I told you that I love him, it would be an understatement. I have seen some rather hot guys here and I hope I can resist the temptation.

I never thought I would say this and now I'm writing it down on paper … Lebanon is a beautiful country, with scenic views and mountainous terrain. The people, on the other hand, I beg to differ: even though they are hospitable and have such yearning desires to feed you constantly that I can't breathe, they smother you and like to control your every move. But on the flipside, I'm reasonably content, for now anyway. I have also discovered ample facts about my Druze religion and that will be the new focus of my energies and getting a job.

University is out of the question, and to be accepted I have to complete year twelve again to meet their standards. I'm sure you know my thoughts on that one!

My uncle Essam said there are a lot of teaching jobs on offer – they love fluent speaking Australians, no need for qualifications and may start me at younger school level age children with low pay, but I figure it's better than staying home doing nothing.

I will definitely keep you posted on the progress of my stay here in 'Lebo Land' and please do the same, like if you happen to bump into NE, tell him I'm thinking about him and give him my address. It's a small world out there so you never know who you may accidently cross paths with. The same goes with CA. I genuinely hope you see him – at least one of us deserves to get the man of our dreams! And more importantly, please don't forget to check the newspaper to see if I got into my chosen preference at university, perhaps then my dad can see the light and come back to Melbourne. Anyway, don't be a stranger and send a letter my way (ASAP).

Yours truly, missing you more than words … your best friend for life.

Sarah xxoo

Sarah folded her neatly written letter and placed it in the envelope, rather enjoying sealing it with the tip of her tongue and gathering that sweet glue-like taste in her mouth.

Nabila walked into the room. 'What are you doing Sarah? Come and have something to eat.'

Sarah cleared her throat. 'Yeah, I'm famished. I just finished writing a letter to my best friend Leila back home.'

Looking at her with sympathy and understanding, Nabila said, 'You look like you miss home.' She gently rubbed Sarah's back. 'Now come, we have something to eat, we made your favourite tabouli and chicken rice with all those glorious nuts on top!'

'I'm beginning to salivate, that's absolutely my favourite and now I feel guilty that I didn't help with any preparation.' Sarah grinned cheekily.

Nabila rolled her eyes and tried to hide her amusement. 'Yeah, we could have done with some extra hands to cut the parsley, perhaps you can help with the washing up instead just to earn your keep!'

Sarah nudged Nabila and they giggled whole-heartedly, bringing their bond even closer.

# Chapter Seventeen

Sarah greeted the chill of the morning coupled with thoughts of Spencer, imagining to be in his warm embrace. This was short-lived and dispelled with Jamal thumping on her bedroom door with, 'Wake up *ya* Sarah, *yallah*! We can't keep our guests waiting.' Jamal repeated this line many times. Sarah knew for sure that the tone in her mothers' voice was one of wedding bells in the air, so she pulled her doona over her head and tried to block out the noise, rather like the sound of a siren resonating across a harbor.

Sarah turned to see if Nabila was awake, but she did not budge and seemed in a deep state of sleep. Sarah wanted desperately to ignore her mother but thought she would go on like a broken record anyway, so Sarah groaned like a sick dog while mumbling obscenities under her breath. 'Yes Mum, okay! I hear you … I'm coming just let me get dressed.'

Jamal seemed happy now; her manner reduced to a sweetness as she replied, 'Good girl *habibti*, *yallah* Sarah, we are waiting.'

Sarah half-heartedly heaved out of bed and looked at herself in the mirror. She didn't like the vision before her – she never did really, as she felt she always looked rotund and somewhat like a puffer fish in desperate need to be deflated. She pondered that thought for a while and then something ingenious struck her; for once, she was in good spirits and breathed a sigh of relief. Sarah spoke to herself, 'Why the hell should I look good or presentable for this guy? I should be pleased I don't look so appealing.'

With that in mind, Sarah figured if she looked more like a boy, perhaps he would be less impressed and thus her parents wouldn't want to encourage the idea of marriage; hence, her plane ticket back to Auzzie-land seemed within reach, she envisaged.

Sarah looked in the wardrobe for some sporty looking outfits she frisked through them and there it was, the ensemble she was looking for: Nike running shoes with a cool looking cap to top it off. Sarah rolled her hair in a bun low enough to place the cap on comfortably and a sense of victory consumed her.

Sarah looked down and noticed Nabila's smug look. 'Sarah, are you going out like that?' Nabila said sleepily. 'You'll be the talk of the town surely!'

'No, I'm not … not before I put some gum in my mouth!' Sarah huffed and chewed intensely. Nabila looked shocked but made no effort to stop her.

Sarah walked proudly into the lounge were the guests were seated. As soon as Sarah approached, the guests stood up and she continued to chew while shaking each one's hand. As she met her mother's eyes, she knew Jamal was plotting to kill her! Sarah ignored Jamal as she motioned to remove the cap, received the guests with a warm smile and was seated.

Sarah noticed one of the visitors was a sheikha, as her head was covered with a white fabric; Sarah was immediately intrigued but felt perhaps she would wait for the right moment before probing about her mysterious religion. The sheikha looked at Sarah, eyes travelling the length of her, and she nodded before she spoke in an articulate grace. 'Welcome to Lebanon, Sarah! You like Lebanon or Australia better?'

Sarah didn't know how to answer that question without offending anyone, so she replied as she would when she was much younger when someone would ask her who she liked better – her mum or dad: she would often reply 'both' without hesitation and knew she would be in no trouble with that answer.

Sarah redirected her gaze to the older looking gentleman seated next to the woman and assumed it had to be her husband. Sarah interjected and chewed impolitely, 'I can see this is your husband – but why, I must ask, is he not in full attire, I mean sheikh clothing?' Sarah knew she had a slight case of foot in mouth disease and didn't know where she was going with that question, but blurted it out before thinking.

'Oh no, Sarah, this man is my son, Adel, and he is looking for a good girl to call his wife!' She was close enough to nudge Sarah in a humorous manner, hugging her and squeezing her shoulder. She laughed heavily enough for the whole room to join in.

Sarah sank in her chair and wished she could curl up under a rock as all eyes were on her.

Finally Marrouf broke the merriment and addressed Adel, who was well dressed in a smart suit and blazer, which made him look much more mature – or perhaps his receding hairline made him look all the more older to Sarah. 'Adel, so what do you do for a living and did you complete university?' The room was silent and all (including Sarah) waited for a response.

He shifted in his chair a little. 'I work as an accountant and I attended Lebanese university where I completed my degree, Bachelor of Commerce and Business Administration, majoring in accounting.'

Sarah was amazed at how well and quickly he spoke English but hoped to God her parents wouldn't force her into marrying this guy, as even the very thought made her sick in the stomach.

Adel turned to face Sarah and was direct in his statement; his voice did not match his strong features, being of high pitch and raspy undertones. 'You're sportive! I like that!'

Sarah frowned, thinking that wasn't the impression she wanted to give – at least not a good one in which Adel clearly stated he liked. She also didn't want to correct his English, thinking if he meant 'sporty' rather than 'sportive' (meaning playful and light-hearted). All the same, she didn't want to impress him in the least, and hoped her being nervous and a little on edge didn't give Adel signals she was interested.

Jamal waved her hand in a quick motion for Sarah's eyes only and she followed her mother into the kitchen, where Jamal was making black coffee for the guests. As pleased as she was to escape the bad atmosphere, Sarah held her breath in anticipation of Jamal's attack and judgment based on her clothing.

'Sarah, you embarrass me! Why don't you dress nice and feminine, as a lady should? You know very well your father and I are not going to leave Lebanon until you are married! You should have made an effort, as Adel is very well educated and has a good job, and his father owns many apartments and land. It is a respectable family and he is an only child, so you know that Adel will get all his father's inheritance. Sarah, you have already rejected so many men so now your father and I are going to make decision for you!'

'Mum … what are you saying, that I don't even have a choice in the matter? It's my life and I don't think it's ethical, we have only exchanged a few words!'

'Sarah, *habibti*, when you are engaged you will have plenty of time to get to know one another. Now go Sarah, here's the tray of coffee, go now, offer our guests, eldest first remember!' Jamal forced her forward with a little jab on Sarah's back and swiftly pulled her cap off her head, loosening Sarah's nicely twisted bun.

Sarah complied with Jamal only because she knew she had to derive a plan. Dan sneered with a glint of dark, malevolent eyes, which made Sarah all the more furious. Sarah wished she could run away right there and then, and the lump in her throat throbbed as she suffered the pain which was all too familiar when she felt powerless or upset. As Sarah's inner voice implored her to get up, she didn't run; she barely even moved. She just sat there motionless, listening to all the interchanges around her without really focusing on what was said. All Sarah could recall was her mother's words replaying over and over again in her mind. She even noticed Dan having a wonderful chat with Adel; her brother made animated facial expressions. He looked like he was enjoying the conversation with Mr Potential Brother-in-law.

Adel then looked at his mother and nodded, giving her the gesture to leave as he put down his finished coffee and gave humble words of thanks for their hospitality. Adel stood up and Marrouf didn't hesitate to invite Adel and the rest of his family for dinner the following day, which Adel gratefully accepted without much thought or deliberation.

# Chapter Eighteen

The morning had delivered a loud hammering on the front door, just before the stroke of noon. Not the usual rat-a-tat-tat, but that of striking blows even the neighbours would have heard.

Sarah noticed Dan run to the door and swing it open. She thought it must be Adel and his family but to her relief and realizing they had invited Adel for dinner, not lunch – it was in fact her cousin Zane.

It wasn't the first time Sarah had met him; he looked in his early forties and Sarah thought him to be quite handsome for his age. Zane was tall and of solid build, and had the sweetest green eyes you could drown in for hours, and when he smiled his eyes gleamed which emphasised them all the more. Sarah looked at him puzzled, thinking he was coming over more regularly lately and wondered what his motives were – he usually liked to speak with Marrouf in private. Sarah recalled Zane was an engineer, so the need for money seemed out of the question. Subsequently, he rarely brought his wife and kids and Sarah felt there must be some private business between himself and her father. Sarah's theory was right, as she overheard Marrouf and Zane talking about a business venture they would team together as a partnership.

Marrouf hurried to the door and stretched his arm in greeting. '*Ahlan, ahlan* Zane, my favourite nephew … have you found a business we could lease?' Marrouf always cut to the crunch and got straight to the point.

Zane smiled quite charmingly and said in his charismatic way, 'Indeed uncle! It's in Aley, which is central between Beirut and the mountains.'

'Good, very good – we will have a look at it tomorrow, as tonight we have guests in particular for Sarah! If you'd like to stay for dinner, you are most welcome.'

Zane agreed and Sarah wasn't happy, thinking if this partnership did go to plan she wouldn't have much luck leaving Lebanon anytime soon. Zane looked down at Sarah and winked. 'Congratulations, *mabrook* Sarah!' Zane shook Sarah's hand vigorously before Sarah could deny his assumption. Marrouf then lead Zane into the guest room.

Dan mocked in his evil way at Sarah before uttering while pointing to his ring finger, 'Sarah's getting married to Adel! Ha ha …' Dan said obnoxiously.

Sarah felt her insides churning and was going to hit him before she noticed Jamal's shadow through the hallway and whispered under her breath, 'I'll get you back for that, you prick, you really think I'm gonna marry someone like that? For God's sake!'

Sarah then crept her way into the guest room, remaining unseen to eavesdrop on her father's conversation. Sarah didn't like what she heard: Marrouf was going to give Zane ten thousand American dollars to start up the electrical and building supply business, and they would equally share in the profits. Marrouf didn't know anything about electrical cables or the like.

Sarah wondered how it would work but knew deep down how stubborn and strong-minded Marrouf was – that once he put his mind to something, no one could stand in his way. Sarah understood now the reason Jamal didn't get involved with decisions he made and to argue; it would be like hitting her head against a brick wall. Evidently Jamal went with the flow of the passing current.

As for Sarah, she didn't want to be like Jamal at all – and the first thing she had to do to achieve this was reject any marriage proposals. If she had no say in that, Sarah would have to go with the treacherous tide – for now, anyway, although her patience ran thin as she seethed with frustration.

Jamal called Sarah to help with the coffee making, which seemed an endless and daily chore. She thought she would use the opportunity to see if Jamal knew anything about Zane's so-called business proposition.

'Mum, did you know anything about Dad and Zane going into business together? There's always a motivation for people and for Zane to come around so often ...'

Jamal nodded and very slowly said, 'You know your father, and I think it will be good for him to get out of the house and keep busy. It's better than him playing cards till all hours of the morning and gambling his money away. This is a good business venture for us all, investing in a business for money growth – otherwise it will slip through our fingers and our money will fall into decline, leaving us no other choice but to go back to Auzzie-tralia.'

Sarah didn't reply and was silently quite pleased with going back to Australia, and felt she shouldn't worry about anything. God had a plan in place that Sarah thought would work out to her benefit. She just had to keep her faith alive. Indeed, this was instilled in her from an incredibly young age – the love of some peaceful strengthening entity that was looking out for her.

Sarah knew Marrouf would submit to Zane's proposition and that it would work out for only a short time. One thing she was not sure of was how the dinner with Adel would pan out; she was worried about how the evening would conclude. Sarah didn't have a plan and didn't want to burden her mind about it. She knew that whatever God had in mind for her was already written and whichever path she took would lead to the same outcome – secretly hoping her journey would lead to Spencer.

Adel and his family, along with his five year old cousin Wael, came and had dinner as expected. Sarah was happy to chat with this young lad and his aunty said that Wael remembered his afterlife – Sarah took great interest asking many questions with utmost fascination. 'So little man, tell me what you remember about your former life. As your aunt said, you remember your family in your past life?' Sarah exclaimed.

The child looked at Sarah with astute knowing eyes, lifted his checked shirt and pointed to his birthmark located on his chest; he spoke in a scholarly fashion. 'See! Sarah, see the mark? My parents think it's a birthmark but in fact, it's a gunshot wound. That's where I was shot with a handgun!'

She looked in disbelief and entertained the thought. 'Shot, really? Why, how?'

Wael could barely stay still and he punctuated his speech with wild gesticulations. 'I was fighting with my neighbour George, who fancied my wife. She told me this man was harassing her so I threw a punch and that's how it all started. He just shot me before I had a chance to pull out my own long arm rifle. I had two children, you know, and a beautiful wife – she was the most attractive lady in the whole village.'

'Oh really, and what are their names?' Sarah asked sceptically with a slight giggle.

'Hebba and Ramsey – my wife's name was Jasmine.'

Sarah fired many questions at Wael and discovered that he recalled his past life in astonishing and extensive detail, to the extent of naming his village where he and his family had resided. He recited events and facts about his previous life, including incidents, people, places, food and clothes; even Dan was deeply intrigued by Wael and his story sparked interest with the whole family, even surprising his own family with new details.

Adel mentioned that at first they thought it was all in Wael's imagination or inventiveness, but with all the proof and comprehensive research, it confirmed vivid memories of a past life. Conversely, Marrouf cast a shadow and darkened all in high spirits; he interrupted, 'Okay, *ahlan* Adel! We invited you this evening to give you good news. Sarah has agreed to your proposal of marriage. I suspect you will give my daughter some time before the wedding is arranged to get to know you better.'

Sarah's heart sank in sheer terror and she sat there in a paralysed state in silence. She felt her face flush and her body trembled, but she couldn't conjure up any courage to refute Marrouf.

Adel smiled and seemed pleased; his voice ripened to a lower tone than his usual high pitch. 'Uncle Marrouf, you name how much gold; I mean nothing is too much for Sarah! Anything for my lovely girl.' Adel looked at Sarah, his face gleaming with gratification. All the while Sarah frowned; she was certain it was apparent that she wasn't happy. However, Adel did surprise her then and he stood up suddenly, focusing his attention to Marrouf. 'Sarah and I want to have a few words alone, if you'll excuse us … if you don't oppose this Uncle, do I have your approval?'

Marrouf nodded unwillingly with what looked like a spasm of pain contorting his face. 'As you like.'

Sarah escorted Adel to a private living room area and she observed how tall he was, a little over six foot tall and lanky. They both were promptly seated. Sarah was in casual clothing as she was keeping to the 'boy look' theme; Adel wore a classy, remarkably tailored suit with smart cuff links and all, looking like an authentic groom.

'Sarah, I wanted to be alone with you, as I felt when your dad mentioned you accepted my proposal … well, you didn't seem happy at all! I don't have to be a rocket scientist to know perhaps your parents forced you to accept me.'

Sarah tried hard not to lose her temper. 'Adel … look, you're right and what you're saying is an understatement really, as my parents didn't even have the common decency to ask me about my feelings. I didn't even know you proposed.'

'Look Sarah, before you continue and I can see you're upset, you know you may not like me now, but we can grow to love one another slowly, slowly … you know, like Charles and Lady Diana did. Have you heard the story that Charles was in love with another woman before he met Diana? Nonetheless they grew to love each other.'

Sarah couldn't believe her ears and wanted to laugh so hard that she almost couldn't contain herself; she was internally in deep hysterics. 'That's a classic story and very interesting Adel, but let's just be friends for now okay?'

Adel looked at Sarah in that instance with an intense evil glare that plunged her into a deep silent horror. His eyes looked so large, enhancing those spectacles on his face; the timing was spot on as Jamal walked into the room and broke the ice that stood between her and the man she was supposed to marry. Sarah was relieved to hear her father was waiting for her, as she didn't enjoy the company of this particular stranger.

She couldn't fathom her parents' reckoning – their codes of ethics or their dictates of conscience. Sarah was utterly disgusted with her parents and couldn't look at them with the sheer admiration she did in her childhood years.

# Chapter Nineteen

Sarah was surprisingly happy with the news and arrival of a long awaited letter; Nabila was the one to do the honours as she handed it over enthusiastically. 'Look Sarah, a letter from your best friend – sender says Leila Mettar, Melbourne, Victoria.'

Sarah couldn't hold back her glistening smile and tears welled up around the corners of her eyes. She was happy to learn the letter was from Leila, her most treasured friend; however, in her heart she hoped there would be some news of Spencer – that he missed her and was waiting patiently for her return. Sarah opened the envelope with childlike fervour, like a child opening the wrapper of a well-earned chocolate bar.

To my dearest friend Sarah,

I miss you so much can you believe how time has flown by ... It's been six months already. Anyway, thank you so much for your long awaited letter, I had almost given up on you.

Well, life in Auzzie-land is pretty much the same as you left it with the exception of the fact I didn't get into the uni I applied for. My lovely mum forced me to repeat year twelve again; I don't mind as I really want to do business management, so one extra year won't kill me as we're halfway through the year anyway.

I have enclosed a section of The Age that clearly states
you got into Deakin University to study a double degree in
secondary teaching and arts, which I'm sure you'll be happy to
hear and congrats on that!

I know what's on your mind, but I'd rather start talking about
CA first before I get stuck into who you're dying to hear about,
cause that's where your interest lies. To cut a long story short,
I did see CA. BEAUTIFUL guy! He is working part time at my
local video store, can you believe that? Fate, I tell you, and
guess what? He asked about what I was doing with myself, if
I got into uni, etc. I was so embarrassed and tongue-tied but
I told him the truth and he was unbelievably empathetic and
understanding. Anyway, it really made my day seeing him even
though he didn't ask for my phone number ...

I know what you're thinking and I didn't see NE, but a certain
someone in your English Lit class did, and she called me
asking about you, and that NE and herself want to catch up
with you for lunch one day, apparently he's still single and very
keen on you. Celine Achen actually thinks NE is interested
in her but we both know the answer to that one. He would
always favour you over her and everybody knew you were the
special one, the class pet. I told Celine you're in Lebanon at the
moment and I'll be sure to let her know when you hit home soil.
Oh the memories!

Anyway, what I'm trying to tell you is hurry up ... get back to
where your heart is before your man's affections find another
... but I doubt that will happen anytime soon. So I'm sure you
have devised a plan and if you need any assistance from me,
I'll help you in any way from my part of the world. Oh, and by
the way before I forget, NE is no longer working at our school
... apparently he's currently a lecturer at Melbourne uni, talk
about going up in the world!

Look after yourself Sarah! Take care ... till we meet again very soon ...

Your bestie Leila xxoo

PS. Brad Tanker called me and asked about you! Not that you care but apparently he got into Law at Monash Uni! Surprise, surprise. Who would have thought, 'Thomas the Tank Engine', the boy with the stutter ... Also better tell you that your crush at one stage, Chris Ricardo – now on Australia's most wanted list! I'm serious, not kidding! I guess he figured if he could get any girl he wanted and could flout the law. But I don't want to delve too deeply into his details until we meet, I'll tell you personally. Xx oo mwahhh.

Sarah breathed in and out quickly and her head fell in a downward meticulous motion as she pounded it repetitively on the desk in front of her, her hands covering her face in a cup-like fashion. She thought about Spencer and how she yearned to be with him. Deep down in her heart she knew the sad reality: he wouldn't wait for her forever. He was a man, after all, and the fact that she was so far away ... people change and feelings change, she pondered.

That pint-size negative voice hollered heavily into Sarah's subconscious state yet again. She found it hard to ignore and drop out of the destructive mindset, although that's what distance does to the soul: it yields life to doubt and distrust. Sarah felt the sheer pain of hopelessness without promise.

In the midst of all this frustration, Dan pounced into Sarah's room and spoke in his usual nasally irritating voice. 'Hey Sis, guess what? You got a date with the Devil himself! So Mum told me to tell you to get ready, as today Adel is here waiting for you. He wants to take you to downtown Beirut, or Hamra, to buy you the engagement dress, how exciting for you hey? Okay, get cracking, we don't want to keep the groom waiting and you know how Mum gets all cranky and shaky, so don't take your time!' said Dan with a grin from ear to ear.

Sarah knew too well Dan took great pleasure in her pain and grief. With that in mind she didn't understand her brother's resentment towards her – was it just normal sibling rivalry? She figured it was all just a big game to him. One big joke! 'Okay, calm down, tell Mum I'm coming,' Sarah yelled, grief-stricken and almost throwing the closest object she could find but failing miserably … as per usual.

Sarah got dressed in casual clothing, keeping to her prior theme, and took the 'what the heck' approach to life for now anyway, thinking about Dan and the way he endured life with his childlike mentality. Sarah said to herself under her breath, 'Okay sister, let's just go with the flow, like Mum does with Dad! God will find a way out of this – it's in your hands Lord, heavenly father.'

Sarah always felt less stress when she placed her troubles and undesirable weights onto God's strong shoulders; at least she thought she didn't have to deal with her problems alone.

Sarah walked through the hallway and to her dreaded surprise, found walking in the opposite direction a dark shadow at first, turning into a tall lanky figure – that of Adel himself.

'Oh Sarah *hayete*, my life, you are so lovely. I missed you.' Adel shook her hand and before letting go, squeezed it in a playful manner. Sarah didn't appreciate this motion – unless this gesture had come from Spencer. Just at that precise moment, thinking about the love of her life, her heart sank as Adel came closer to her. 'You are so beautiful like a strong flower, you give me energy. It is very easy for any man to fall in love with you, with all your proactive energy, sensual and sexy and full of joy. This is why, Sarah, I like you too much and have no problem to say I love you – if only you would give me a chance to prove this.'

Adel took off his silver metallic ringed Timberland spectacles and leaned in closer to kiss her. Sarah trembled, wishing Spencer would say those words directly and with so much passion as Adel. She thought how cruel life was, being so far from Spencer. *Distance is such a silent killer,* she thought. Her body flinched backwards almost automatically and the rejection was evident.

However, this did not faze Adel and he grinned, moving away ever so slightly. 'It will take time, till we are both comfortable with each other. You're a good girl and I like that.'

Sarah was speechless and a realisation came over her: this act that she was playing was not going to be an easy task ahead. How could he have developed deep strong feelings and in such a short time? Sarah knew that she was a great catch and would be giving this guy or any other man in Lebanon a ticket, hence the opportunity for a better life in the land of endless prospects and security – 'Auzzie-land'.

Sarah was playing the part of the submissive teenager and her parents seemed pleased, all the while Dan was exchanging sneaky glances as if he could read Sarah like an open book and knew what she was up to. Sarah eyed off Dan like a cold callous killer stalking her victim; she knew Dan felt the intensity of her stare as he retrieved eye contact quickly. She felt more powerful than ever before, proving to herself a mighty dominance as she walked out of the place she now called home; Adel opened the door and paused to allow Sarah to lead.

Sarah smiled with an unpretentious subtleness and held her head high thinking to herself, *I've got to play a strategic game and make Adel believe I will marry him, just like a game of chess.*

# Chapter Twenty

Sarah remained in a positive mindset as she uttered, 'Lebanon was nearing to an end!'

Indeed, her parents made it clear they were unhappy with the current business partnership with handsome cousin Zane. She overheard Marrouf and Jamal quarrelling on numerous occasions.

'Oh Marrouf, how could we possibly leave Lebanon now? It's too soon and Sarah hasn't even signed her marriage certificate, she's only been engaged for a few weeks!'

Marrouf frowned and the lines on his forehead prominent as he lit his Marlboro cigarette. '*Ya* Jamal! Business is very bad in this country with all the debt build-up – people just don't pay up here! We all work very hard in Lebanon for few and minimal wages. People here are have "hang or be hung" mentality, steal or starve frame of mind. This behaviour perhaps learned from the war and poverty. Unlike people in Australia most are honest and afraid to break the law. When I go to their homes here to collect the money owed to us they tear my heart in half, shred it to pieces I tell you!

'I feel I want to give them the clothes off my own back, *ya* Jamal. They send me on a guilt trip and show me their poverty-stricken homes, leaving me no choice but to sympathise with them and their families. We have to stop before we go into bankruptcy … staying in the same predicament will lead us to impoverishment ourselves.

'*Yii ya* Jamal, what's wrong with you! We just don't belong here anymore. I feel like an outsider on my own home soil, I'm getting my share from Zane and we have to leave immediately! Sarah will have to sign the marriage certificate before we leave Lebanon, then we will help Adel with the paperwork arrangements from the Department of Immigration in Australia.'

Jamal sat on the couch, feeling defeated. 'Marrouf, we came here for the sole purpose of getting our children get married so we don't lose control over them in Auzzie-tralia and marry outside our religion. The people will talk and we will get a bad name, *ya* Marrouf.'

'Jamal, Jamal … people will talk regardless, even if we lay red carpet and give them a gold lira for each child they have … you can't satisfy people's need for gossip and idle chatter. Now go tell the children of our plans … we will leave in the next couple of weeks. But mark my words, Sarah will be signing and Adel will be legally her husband in the eyes of Lebanese law.'

Sarah overheard her parents' conversation and could not believe what she was hearing. She was utterly disappointed with her mother's words, yet a joy warmed her spirit. Deep within, Sarah knew it was all God and he was shedding his glorious light on her. Indeed, good things come to those who wait and are patient in life.

She didn't care about signing the marriage certificate; after all, it was a measly piece of paper, she reassured herself. All that was on her mind was going back to the country she adored and the one person she loved with every grain of her existence.

News, as all news in Lebanon, travelled quickly: the Basheer family was heading back to Australia. There were tears and sadness amongst relatives; Sarah shed tears of sheer pleasure and all the decayed inherent feelings seemed to escape and disperse from her body.

Sarah reminisced in fury about her small engagement gathering to husband-to-be Adel, the resentment she felt towards her parents and every one of her relatives that joined in celebration. Arabic dancing and horrid high pitched ululation tongue trills – 'Ah-weeeee-ha' – and the Zalghouta to mark ceremony. Showered with what seemed like her entire weight in gold, with an exquisite dress and makeup to a flawless perfection, Sarah felt indeed like a princess. But she was overwhelmed with guilt, as she wished it were Spencer by her side. All the money, gifts or inheritance couldn't satisfy Sarah's pursuit for happiness with a man she did not love or share any kind of bond with. She couldn't change the past and was looking forward to unravelling her future upwelling of hope and prosperity.

Sarah couldn't contain or hide the smile on her face and as Jamal approached grimacing, observing her daughter with knowing eyes as she involuntarily gave her word of Marrouf's decision. Sarah wanted to jump out of her skin and knew her mother sensed her inner delight – much to Jamal's dismay and feeling of defeat.

'Sarah, my only daughter, don't thinka for one second you have won as we are going back to Auzzie-tralia, but mark my words you will be signing the marriage certificate and you will have to respect Adel and follow your husband. This is the life, Sarah … we are Druze! He is wealthy and may want to reside in Lebanon, so take a mental note of that … no girl of mine is going back to her boya-friend and naughty girls that are like bad rotten apples! You understand you can't blacken our name. I forbid it!' Jamal raised her index finger and Sarah noticed her hands shaking and intense fury in her eyes, which usually looked placid and kind.

Sarah was speechless and knew her mum meant business. She swallowed her breath and didn't want to thrust any more kerosene on the subject to fuel the already sweltering furnace that was Jamal. 'Mum, I understand – relax and don't worry. I like Adel: he has not only got money but he is a true gentleman, kind with a generous, gracious spirit… I think he may be my soul mate and I'm happy to sign my life over to Adel. Just be calm Mum, I want to make you happy before myself. I'm not interested in any Auzzie guys nor do I have a boyfriend.'

Jamal warmed and settled calmly; Sarah was pleased to observe this as she didn't like to see her mother agitated or upset. *I have to lie if it's going to make Mum happy and less stressed.* Sarah walked merrily to her room to start packing that wonderful vintage suitcase – oh how she loved that op shop luggage now, especially with the welcomed destination forthwith.

Sarah reflected on past school classes with Spencer, the memories sparking a fervour that made her smile. She conjured up all the embedded feelings of divine love that eased her negative thoughts and self-doubts. Her visions of Spencer resonated real and true, like he was right there in the same room watching her. Sarah loved it when those remarkable blue eyes would follow her, like he was looking right into her soul and drawing all her insecurities, leaving her feeling in high spirits.

How could this be? A love so strong without declaration … Sarah pondered having an existing relationship only built on mere feelings, words, analysis and signs. Without touch, actions, affection or intimacy that couples often take for granted. How could a soul yearn for another indirectly? Sarah couldn't fathom. She could only hope Spencer felt the same way and she was going to find out one way or another. At long last Australia seemed within her reach; if only she could grasp it soon. Sarah could taste its tantalising delights.

Dan ran into Sarah's room and didn't stop to knock or excuse his abrupt manner; Sarah perceived Dan to be without a courteous bone in his scrawny body; he was like his mother Jamal – tall, attractive and flawless – but beauty ran only skin-deep in his case.

Dan resumed teasing, with a moment's pause to snicker slyly. 'Hey Sarah! I bet you're over the moon about the news, if you haven't heard? Dad said you still have to marry Adel whether you like it or not! And you know sis, I'm a bit happy about that. So delighted, in fact, that we're going back to Auzzie-land. I'm sick of the fake, phony and unoriginal gals here. Only good for a one night stand, if they'd let you! Damn political virginity in this country! Although the "married ones" are … ooohh, must I say more?

'So thank God that I don't have to get married like you! And no longer have to deal with electricity shortages, or having to boil water in an ancient metal vessel just to have a bloody shower. I miss drinking milk straight out of a carton, our general infrastructure and lifestyle back home. Hmmmm, I guess you don't care cause you're only thinking about your husband Adel!'

Sarah couldn't be bothered making a comeback or satisfying Dan with a response. She inhaled deeply and counted to five in reverse. Showing her anger was exactly what he wanted – and besides, Sarah was too happy, thinking she could soon reunite with Spencer finally.

She resorted to a simple shrug and huff, while Dan looked knocked for six and stumbled out of the room feeling thwarted.

# Chapter Twenty-one

A solitary tear, but one of many, slid down Sarah's face as she bid farewell to her favourite cousin, Nabila. They embraced for a long while, both being consciously aware of the strong bond they shared. Nabila announced, eyes welling up with tears, 'I'd just gotten used to my roommate, now you're going to leave me Sarah – I'm gonna miss you so much! You're like a sister to me.'

Sarah blushed. 'Oh Nabila *habibti*, me too, honey – don't worry, we will keep in contact and I will try to write to you every day or as often as possible. Hmmm, perhaps you can start writing that translation of our precious *Kitab al-Hikma*, thy "Book of Wisdom", if you happen to get your hands on it, ha ha!' Sarah said.

Nabila looked around discreetly as family members gathered for the formal farewell dinner and marriage signing; rich aromas of Lebanese cuisine were ever present and a little distracting as Sarah's tummy churned.

'It's interesting you brought that up, Sarah! As I have a little present for you – gift wrapped, so don't open it until you are on the aeroplane, okay? Please, promise me that … and there's a little note attached inside explaining all you need to know … hush, hush, now take it and not another word Sarah, okay?' Nabila slid the package into Sarah's heavy woollen coat pocket and patted it gently. 'Guard it with your life, dear sister, and no questions now, please!'

Sarah swallowed her hunger and knew exactly what it was, but respected Nabila's wishes – even though with every inch of her being wanted so desperately to rip it open right that instant for a true beaming revelation. Sarah breathed. 'Okay my dear sister, I am rather tempted and patience is not one of my strong points, but I respect your wishes.'

Nabila winked and could not hold back as her emotions got the better of her, hands trembling as she tried to wipe away her tears. 'I'm so sorry Sarah, I know how happy you are to be going back to your country and your friends and I'm happy for you, really … I know you were struggling here, with no work, study or that sense of belonging. Don't worry, I know how you feel; I'm with you, *hayete*! Good luck in your travels, I sincerely hope you find what you're looking for. It may very well be right under your nose!'

Sarah smiled fondly; she was too emotional, grasping the gift ever so slightly in her fleece pocket as she wept quietly. 'Thank you Nabila, I am indebted to you truly. I don't know how I could have survived here without you in this country.'

Sarah turned, regaining composure, and said her goodbyes to the rest of her relatives before breathing a gentle sigh of relief – well, for a short time anyway, before she came face to face with Adel. He looked at her with his usual intensity that frightened her; she wasn't intimidated, but nevertheless she was taken aback like a sail being pressed against the mast by an overpowering headwind. 'Sarah my love, the sheikh is here for the marriage signing. Come now, we will eat and then our love and mutual binding will be signed, sealed and delivered.'

Sarah flashed him an insincere smile and seated herself where Adel signalled; she dutifully accepted, knowing it was only one more day of this torture and then she would be free. Sarah remained cool and had lost her appetite rather quickly, as that all too familiar lump in her throat grew sore and tender. Sarah frisked her food with her fork around the plate, much to young Wael's amusement, who was sitting directly opposite from Sarah. He mimicked her movements and giggled gloriously like a jolly old fellow as Sarah blushed. She adored Wael and wished it were possible she could adopt him; with those sweet irresistible chubby cheeks he looked so innocent and childlike, but his soul in contrast seemed omniscient and wise.

Sarah would often joke with Wael if he would like to accompany her to Australia – he would fit quite comfortably nestled in her vintage suitcase. His reply was always, 'Sarah, I have money! I have no problem buying a ticket so I can sit right beside you, *ya habibti.*'

All that occurred early that day was quite vague, with the exception of Jamal placing the white sheikha cloth over Sarah's head as she signed her life away, but not in Sarah's mindset; she always had a backup plan.

Three cars filled with friends and relatives escorted Sarah and her family for their flight departure – or, for Sarah's want of a better word, 'aircraft saviour'.

Sarah's heart skipped a beat, thinking both of how much closer she was to Spencer and the prospect of unravelling Nabila's precious gift she held intrinsically close to her. As they boarded the plane, Sarah thought she would wait for just the right moment, even though she was straining at the leash to open it. Sarah didn't hesitate as she boarded the aircraft; she was in high spirits and her smile exuded her happiness, as she felt free at long last.

Sarah waited a while until she felt it was safe to open Nabila's present; luckily Jamal chose to sit next to Sarah in the middle aisle as Dan preferred the window seat next to Marrouf. She figured if she could remain as far away as possible from her treacherous brother, all would be good.

She carefully slit the decorative packaging with her index finger to reveal firstly the note attached with her name on it; Sarah eagerly began to read.

To dearest Sarah,

If you're reading this note, you're probably already on the plane right now and smiling. All the while I'm sitting in the room we shared, feeling empty and lonelier than ever, but I know that you are happy and you can now breathe easier as you are almost there sister! Yes, I spent many sleepless nights and countless days translating not all but many parts of our most treasured possession, the 'Book of Wisdom', as it's a corpus of sacred texts, or pastoral letters some may call it. It was tricky to translate cryptic phrases but I tried my best … please let me know how you go with my interpretation and your own valued analysis.

Always in my thoughts and prayers yours truly,

Nabila xox

PS. By the way, if you're a bit curious as to how I got my hands on this sacred text, well … from your one and only, most adorable and charming Wael! Yes, the 'reincarnated chosen one' himself. He told me he swiped it from his aunt (as she is a sheikha) just for you, and I explained you needed it for research purposes. He willingly obliged to assist. So you can thank clever Wael at another point in time.

Hopefully if you're ever around our village, you can personally thank us cause I miss you already. xxoo

Sarah folded the note at once and pulled out Nabila's translated composition in eager anticipation, kissing it excitably. Warmth circled her internally, like fruit of a sort of mystic inspiration. She flicked through it briefly, scanning the pages, but her mind couldn't stay focused and her head and eyes felt heavy as she dozed, perhaps as she knew she was heading in a direction that would lead her to Spencer.

Sarah awoke with slight air turbulence and gathered she must have slept at least a couple of hours. She looked over to her family; they were all in deep sleep. She heard the airline hostess shuffle past her. Sarah realised the book was still in her hand and held it tighter, delving into it like she would chocolate pudding. She read the seven principles, as Nabila noted:

1. *Truthfulness – love of honesty and integrity.*
2. *Comradeship – looking after one another.*
3. *Abandon false beliefs.*
4. *Refrain from evil.*
5. *Accept divine unity in humanity.*
6. *Accept all al-Hakim's acts.*
7. *Surrender in accordance to al-Hakim's will.*

Sarah reflected on these values; she understood 1, 2, 4 and 5 were pretty straightforward. Number 3: rejecting polygamy and slavery. 6 and 7: acceptance, surrender and contentment – 'what will be, will be'.

Consequently, defining the notion that fate will decide the outcome of a course of events, even if action is taken to try to alter it. Hence, yielding and submitting to the unity and will of God and to serve through good deeds.

Surely all religious manuscripts were in fact leading us on the same virtuous path and loyalty to God – that is, the path to avoid evil and live in support of one another. We are indeed a generation of hope. Why then, she considered, must her own religious faith, the creed she was born into, be concealed?

Sarah quickly tucked the book in her pocket in case anyone was to sight her most prized possession; she believed her journey to Lebanon was a worthwhile one. One of sheer simplicity. Had she stumbled on the ending to suffering and war? The notion of 'world peace' diminished at the utterance of the preposterous birth of religion, whose only purpose was subtraction, separation, ostracism, oppression and a world kept in sheer horror and desperation to acquire peace.

This was a light bulb moment of spiritual awakening and self-enlightenment. Sarah had the prodigious 'Book of Wisdom' in the palm of her hand, so to speak. She giggled aloud in a childish manner, the way she envisioned Mozart would mock Salieri as his music phrased harmonious symphonies, composing string quartets and quintets in her mind amidst unwavering delight.

She couldn't fathom how silly she was even to begin decoding the cryptic game and all the wisdom and teachings this sacred text held dear. Sarah considered that most earthlings were undeniably asleep and all religious transcripts preach some form of love of humanity. It is only love that keeps us sane in this insane world.

For the first time in her life, she felt awake and spiritually prepared. She was conscious of an awareness stemming and tugging at her very core, a deep-rooted reckoning.

Sarah wrote:

> Why do we search for some powerful force to cling onto? At birth, isn't it almost an automatic reaction that a single mortal hand rouses us to grip firmly to the warmth of a solitary finger?

> 'God'? Or an entity to grasp onto. Some guiding force to lead us?

> If in fact we inter-be, delve internally, God is us. The sooner we recognise and awaken to the deed, we are all twigs from the same tree, and thenceforth undeniably, we can co-exist together in harmony and grow as one!

# Chapter Twenty-two

'We have reached our final destination: Melbourne, Australia, partly cloudy with a few showers today ... Melbourne weather indeed,' the airline pilot announced on loudspeaker.

Sarah exhaled all her fears and anxieties. *Oh, how I love Melbourne weather – it's so good to be back on Auzzie land and soil!*

Dan looked at Sarah, giving her one of his usual frowns. 'Don't worry, Short-arse Sardines, Adel is sure to be on the next flight to meet you and claim you for his own.'

Sarah shrugged. 'Why are you so worried? No need to vent your concern about Adel ... do you think I look worried?'

Dan looked into Sarah's eyes and almost automatically looked at her hands to see if she was wearing the wedding band Adel had given her at the marriage signing. Sarah had in fact 'misplaced' it and Dan realised this, but to Sarah's amazement he didn't say a word, only gasping loudly, but her parents were too busy arguing over what food they had declared.

'*Ya* Jamal! Why did you bring olives, vine leaves, herbs and spices? We have all these things here! We haven't stated it on these passenger cards, now we will have to wait hours at the airport,' Marrouf hollered, jabbing the card with his index finger.

'Don't worry Marrouf, it's only food *habibi*!' replied Jamal in a calm tone.

'*Ya* Jamal! It's what the food carries! Insects and pesticides. Not good! Big no nos.'

Sarah was embarrassed as per usual with her parent's rants in public, nevertheless was happy the focus was neither on her nor Dan and stood there to grin and bear it!

Marrouf was right and they were delayed – all the while, Sarah's patience grew thin. She just wanted to be in familiar territory and the comfort of her bedroom.

She heaved her precious suitcase as they exited the customs zone, while Marrouf and Jamal eagerly looked around for Uncle Farrouk.

Instead, to Sarah's surprise she saw two familiar faces approaching and grinning delightfully. That of Brad, whom had lost a bit of weight and bulked up handsomely, alongside dear Leila.

'Welcome back, bright eyes! We missed you bella,' said Brad in an unusually charming and confident approach. Sarah and Leila embraced each other, tightly holding their tears back.

'How did you guys know of my arrival? I was gonna surprise you! Anyway, thanks heaps for coming. Oh my God! It's so good to be back here! As the saying goes, you don't know what you've got, till it's gone.'

Brad looked at Sarah like he knew exactly what she meant, as he could relate to her theory. Leila giggled as Sarah congratulated Brad on studying law at Melbourne Uni.

'Well, "Thomas the Tank Engine", you'll probably make as much money as the children's series being a well renowned lawyer,' Sarah said playfully as Leila agreed, nodding eagerly.

Brad expressed with amusement, 'At least I didn't say I want to be like the fricken Fat Controller. That would have got me into heaps more trouble with Mr Fitz, or should I say Mr Gay Lord!'

Sarah was not impressed. 'Well, Brad, I can see you've lost your stutter! Much love and credit to your speech therapist,' she retorted.

'Ah ha! That's it! I knew you had a thing for Mr Fitz all along and look at you! You still do!' Brad tapped Sarah's shoulder. 'Don't worry babe, I can help you find him – anything, you name it! I'll do some research for you, to find out if he's single, married, gay, bi or a dominatrix. Oh Sarah, why so glum? Just teasing, baby! Anything, you name it!'

'Thanks Brad, but no thanks. All's good, don't worry – I have to concentrate on myself at the moment. And look, here come my parents. Brad, just say you're Leila's cousin please, okay?'

'Your whim is my desire!' Brad said smoothly with a little bow.

Sarah reminisced about Spencer and even thought she saw him at the airport that very day; she wasn't sure if it was coincidental or her mind playing tricks on her, but this person looked like Spencer and even walked like him. Sarah wanted so desperately to call out his name as he turned the corner and felt so flustered thinking how deep her feelings were for him still.

Was it pure infatuation? Was Sarah in love with the idea of 'love' or the ideal person she envisioned Spencer to be? How could she possibly know? Just like her 'Book of Wisdom', she held it firmly in her hand and heart – nonetheless, did she really know the secrets deep within? Who was Spencer really? So many questions had Sarah doubting herself and her feelings.

A couple of weeks had passed and an unexpected phone call from Brad had Sarah in high spirits. Old feelings for Spencer resurfaced as Brad expressed that he did some research on Spencer, and found that he was still living with his parents and was indeed single. Brad mentioned if she wanted his details he would happily pass them on to her, on one condition: Sarah would agree to have coffee with him first. Sarah knew there was always a catch, some ulterior motive behind Brad's request, so she declined and told Brad that she had a few issues to deal with at home first. Her future husband Adel's visitor visa application was granted and he would be arriving in the next couple of months for their wedding ceremony, as the signing of marriage was completed prior.

'Sarah, are you sure this is what you want? You know you are over the legal age, you don't have to consent to anything – know your rights! I will help you, I know about the law – Sarah, it's on your side.'

'Thanks Brad, I appreciate what you're saying but I'm happy, really! This is what I want. It may have been an arranged marriage at first, but I have formed strong feelings for this guy. Thank you Brad, for your concern and your trouble, but I told you from the beginning I don't need anyone's help. Goodbye.'

Sarah hung up the phone and guilt plunged over her like an iced water bucket. She knew Brad cared about her and could read her like an open book, but she didn't want any more drama in her life or have to face her problems head-on; it was much easier to surrender, as she held the white flag high enough for her parents to probe with approval.

# Chapter Twenty-three

*Five years later*

Sarah held in her hand a little note with several numbers on it, and she held the telephone receiver in the other; her palms were sweaty. Not a single day had passed without a hint of something that reminded her of Spencer, like love songs on the radio, as well as his presence emerging in her dreams often.

Leila attended the five-year reunion for the graduating class of 93' and all her year level and their teachers were invited, Spencer included. Leila had kindly given her Spencer's phone number that was clearly marked in his handwriting with initials 'SF' on a scrap piece of paper.

Sarah recalled her conversation from earlier that day when Leila had made an unannounced visit.

'Sarah! You should have come to our five year reunion! Everyone rocked up and CA looking more spunky than ever! You wouldn't believe whom I bumped into … yes, NE himself. He seemed so confident and outgoing. It looked like he was looking for you and seemed disappointed when I told him you hadn't come. He was asking so many questions about you, what you were up to. So I had to tell him the truth!'

'Hmmm, so what did you tell him exactly?'

'That you're married to a guy you met in Lebanon and now have a beautiful seven month old baby girl named Miranda. That you're quite successful as your partner has an accounting firm partnered with your dear darling brother Dan. Who would have thought five years ago that would've been the case?'

'You didn't tell Mr Fitz it was an arranged marriage? And I hope you didn't mention my feelings for him?'

'No, not at all, why would I do that? He was so understanding and said it must be quite a handful as having a seven month old is a lot of work, and then handed me this note. I told him I'd give it to you and figured you would call him if you ever had an argument or fight with Adel.'

Sarah drew a sharp breath as she dialled the number. In her mind this wasn't considered cheating; she was only making a simple phone call to a long lost friend, it was in her hands and she had to take it! *Carpe diem*, Sarah deliberated. She wasn't happy in her marriage, after all.

'Hello?' Sarah heard the voice of a mature woman and figured it must be Spencer's mum.

'Hello … could I possibly speak to Spencer Fitzpatrick please?'

'My husband's name is Spencer. Or do you mean Spencer Jnr?'

'Yes, Spencer … Junior. The teacher.' Sarah hesitated and was worried the woman may have heard the tremble in her voice.

'That's okay dear, many people get the two mixed up, ha ha, or perhaps that's just me! Oh, I think he's just stepped out, but just hold the line and I'll check … one moment please, what did you say your name is?'

'Sarah… Sarah Basheer!' Sarah waited and was plagued with self-doubt. Had she made the right decision calling Spencer? What would she say? Was it too late? She didn't want to sound stupid. She considered hanging up the receiver, and then the woman spoke to break Sarah's ambivalent thoughts.

'Yes Dear, thanks for holding, Spencer said he is very pleased you called … ah, here he is now, bye dear.' She handed Spencer the phone.

'Hello?'

'Hello, Mr Fitz ... or may I call you Spencer now?'

'Sarah Basheer! Indeed, how are you, how was Lebanon?' Sarah felt the tenderness in his tone, spirited and energetic.

'I'm really well thanks, and travelling to discover my roots and true essence has sparked some curiosity in me, my religion and faith. Sorry, I shouldn't delve too deeply into this subject right now. You're probably wondering why I'm calling and it has been a while ...'

Spencer intercepted, finishing her sentence. 'It has been a while and perhaps we can chat at a deeper level at some stage? I heard you went to Lebanon shortly after your completion of year twelve, and Leila told me at the reunion that you are married and now have a bundle of joy ... how's life treating you, are you happy?'

Sarah paused for a while and felt the pressure, knowing that Spencer was waiting for at least a quick and honest response, so she felt she had to put her great acting skills into action; she wanted to remain cheerful as that's how he remembered her. 'Yes, really happy thanks! I never thought I'd get married so young, I guess the lucky man swept me off my feet, and now I have a very energetic ankle-biter whom is keeping me on my toes and extremely busy.

'Financially we are doing well as my partner runs his own accounting business with my brother Dan and life is grand, I couldn't really ask for much more. I must admit I had a little crush on you at school ... that's life, I guess it's meant to be complicated. Well, enough about me, I want to know about your life and what you're doing now. Are you engaged, or any romance in the air? I want to know everything! You can start at the point when I graduated and left St Joseph's College.'

Spencer resumed after a slight chuckle. 'Well, firstly I'm not engaged or married and I have had my fair share of short-lived relationships, good ones and bad. Shortly after you completed year twelve, I found myself having to seek alternative teaching jobs and stumbled upon some stroke of luck, you may say, being offered a job as a lecturer at Melbourne Uni – this has bonuses of travelling around the world, particularly as I teach history.'

'That's so great! You deserve it, you were such an inspiration to me and kept the whole class captivated. I thoroughly enjoyed your classes.'

'Thanks Sarah! You and your friends were all an honour to teach.'

The conversation between Spencer and Sarah continued to flow and the spark was ever-present. Sarah really felt a connection, and sensed that Spencer was undeniably her kindred spirit, that she had loved him before in another lifetime.

Spencer was not the type of man to reassure her openly of his feelings or to declare his honest, pure love for her; they were not spoken but nevertheless apparent. He couldn't deny the true fact Sarah was married and couldn't tread on territory that was not his to claim. However, with all this in mind they did arrange to meet and keep it secret, so not even trusty Leila could know of their plans. And who better to babysit than Grandma *teta* Jamal herself?

Sarah hastily rushed to her mother's house, a place she was once ashamed to call home, and as she drove up the driveway, memories of her childhood flashed by her and she wondered that even though she'd lived in a suburb that was not highly regarded and considered 'slums', now she was living in one of the most prestigious parts of town. Was she content or happily married? The answer clearly was no, as she had to bear a hollowness and burning in her heart that she endured daily. Was it God's way of showing Sarah that all the money and luxuries of life couldn't truly buy happiness or love?

Sarah missed her childhood and now that she was older and wiser, she resented her feelings of shame growing up in such an undesirable neighbourhood.

Jamal was always happy to babysit and never really asked Sarah the prying whys or hows, always accepting her granddaughter with open arms coupled with a smile.

'Okay, Mum! Just for a few hours, will $500 suffice?' Sarah thrust the crispy notes onto Jamal's chest along with her baby, formula bottle and baby essentials.

'Eh, Sarah! You look very nice! You going job interview, *habibti*?' Jamal asked inquisitively.

'Yeah Mum, something like that, I won't be long … and don't worry if I'm late, I may swing over to Leila's house.'

# Chapter Twenty-four

Sarah drove on steadily heart in hand, thinking to herself, *follow your heart then your mind will follow*. She wasn't really thinking clearly, trying to stay focused on the road ahead. Sarah allowed herself to be guided by emotion and intuition while her heart began to race. Spencer lived on the outskirts of the city, which was a 45-minute trip for Sarah from her mother's house.

Driving along, she steadily slowed down to discover a lovely picturesque florist, with deep-bronzed wooden flower boxes and red geraniums displayed in pots out front. Nearby, a cat with light and colourful fur was preening itself.

She flipped the gearshift into reverse. Sarah decided that, seeing as she was going to meet Spencer at his parents' place, she would stop off and buy flowers for Spencer's mother, as she didn't want to go there empty handed. Sarah didn't have sound skills at reading maps or the street directory, but she felt that God was guiding her on the right path and in no time had reached her destination.

Sarah drove up the driveway of Spencer's home, number 1805. The entrance was tastefully landscaped with tall bursting vegetation, shrubs and flowers. She liked the number of Spencer's home – particularly the number eight, as she felt it represented infinity and endlessness, hence the love she held deep for Spencer. Could it be a sign of good luck? She hoped so.

Sarah noticed a few cars in the driveway and summoned the courage to ring the doorbell, bouquet of flowers in hand. Its essence exuded, adding calm and comfort as she breathed in its sweet scent.

Who better to answer the door than Spencer himself? His familiar warm smile and deep blue eyes lifted Sarah to heights she couldn't comprehend or explain.

Spencer looked amazing in classy/casual dress attire, even better than Sarah remembered. His eyes caught the lovely cluster of pleasantly arranged flowers. 'Sarah Basheer! Those flowers are beautiful, are they for me? You shouldn't have, really!'

Sarah laughed. 'Actually, Spencer, they're for your mum. Is she here? Do you have guests perhaps?'

'Ah no, my parents are out for the day and my father has a keen interest in classic toys as you may have seen out front. He's a member at the CHACA club. Please come in! Let me look at you.' Spencer grasped Sarah's shoulders. 'You look as lovely as I remember, absolutely ravishing indeed – how old are you now, twenty-two?'

He took the bouquet from her hands and placed them on a side table. Sarah stepped into the alluring entrance and peered around the balanced dainty room, emanating assertive colour tones and textures of the finest furnishings.

'Yes, Spencer, there has always been five years difference between us – you started at St Joseph's so young, right about my age now!'

Spencer gestured towards the sofa, gently placing his hand on the small of her back.

'Spencer, I missed you, you know. I thought about you every day in Lebanon and you really kept me going. I relived moments at school where you made me feel special by inspiring me to be the best version of myself. Your belief in me has shaped a stronger, more determined individual and I came here to thank you for the person I am today. Leila told me to be careful, that teacher/student relationships are unethical and wrong. There always was some impediment standing in our way. I wished though, that deep down you would have said something about your feelings. All just mere speculation on my part … not even a word Spencer, why?'

Her head dropped as though defeated. Spencer moved closer and pinched her jaw, gently edging it towards him as their eyes locked hypnotically. 'I'm not a sleazy teacher who targets teenage girls. You know me! I know my boundaries and codes of conduct. Especially choosing a career in teaching, you have to know where to draw the line.

'Though Sarah … with you, it was different. You are special, unique and your spirit has a gracious captivating energy. I had to suppress my feelings and indeed, it killed me. That's why I didn't express this to you at the time, my teaching career being paramount. Look, I'm only human, but have ethics and morals.

'Sarah, you have a child now and a husband. It's not the right time to change anything, you must continue with your life, that's the choice you made. Life is about choices, good and bad. It's evident you made yours, whatever your reasons may be for doing so. Tell me Sarah, are you in love with your husband?' Spencer grasped her delicate fingers.

Sarah sat in silence and ingested that mischievous ache in her throat. She deliberated, detaching his tender hold. *When is it the right time? Never!* There is always some obstacle, that ever-eventful drama queen called 'Hindrance' that shows up to make life difficult and cause disruption or unrest. *I'm Druze and he's Catholic*, Sarah asserted in her mind. 'Spencer, there's something about me you don't know. Obviously I never could express to you at school that I am Druze.'

Spencer looked on curiously 'Did you say *druid*?'

'No! Druze. A religious sect that stemmed and branched out from the Muslims and their key philosophies.'

'I see. I am deeply intrigued Sarah, though I really don't care what religion you are. I care about you and you alone, it's what's in here that counts.' He stamped his chest in subtle reprise. 'I've never really heard of the Druze religion in all honesty. Did you find yourself closer to your faith in Lebanon?'

'Yes, more than I would've ever expected! I not only surprised myself but my curiosity flourished circulating the Druze and its founders, weaving the omnipresent ether and all four other elements.'

'Wow, Sarah, that's all so impressive. I've heard of the term ether, or air, and it's teaming with an infinitude of small bubbles, in a thick and gluey field as a transmission medium. "The bubbles of nothing, that make it really something". I can aid you in your plight of wisdom, only if you'll let me, as I too have a fascination with religious history. Though you still haven't answered my question. Do you love your husband?'

The evil inner echoes chanted and resonated in the corners of her conscious. Negative forces girdled a beelike swarm of gloom upon her.

The sharp chime of the doorbell sounded suddenly. Sarah was pleased this broke the silence and halted the question at hand, as she didn't want to talk about Adel. She stood up and gazed at Spencer, envisaging it would be the last time she would set her eyes upon him. She'd acted on impulse with the deep, pent-up feelings that she'd bottled up for so long. Too long, in fact, a slow and vanquishing torture.

Spencer grabbed her arm firmly as she reached for the door 'You're not going anywhere Sarah. Not now! I've waited too long to let you go yet again.'

Sarah turned and pulled her arm from Spencer's robust secure hold. She quivered uncontrollably as Spencer pressed her into him ever so intimately, while his lips forcibly cushioned hers in a passionate roaring embrace.

'Let me go! I can't Spencer, I can't do this!' Tears streamed down her face. She gestured towards the crisp light at the 180-degree edge door opening. 'Spencer, I think you should get the door, it may be your parents.'

Spencer grasped the door handle and stared with a look of bewilderment; on the other side there stood Brad Tanker and Celine Achen.

Brad stretched his mouth wide with a grin, holding up a bottle of red and nudged Celine. 'Hey you two!' he said cheekily, extending his hand as he shook Spencer's. We've come to join the party! Mr Fitz Bro, It's been a long time.'

Celine moved forward and pursed her lips on Spencer's cheek, pausing for a while. She turned to Sarah; her eyes seemed filled with a murderous, ravenous hatred. Celine brushed past Sarah and mumbled under her breath as both uninvited guests moseyed on inside.

Sarah wondered, was the arrival of Brad and Celine simply coincidental? Brad knew Sarah's green-eyed monster would rouse at the very mention of her name; it was ever apparent the feelings were mutual.

Sarah had conveyed to Brad at school that Celine had a major crush on Spencer and she hated Celine so much. Sarah detested this element of her own personality – one of jealousy and 'hatred', which was such an angry word. She conceded to the fact this manifest flaw needed to be embraced like a child yearning for support and understanding. This component of her self-needed wisdom and transformation. The toxic seed was already planted and thriving. She burst the poisonous bubble of jealousy with a new-formed perception.

Sarah turned and smiled at Brad and Celine. She uttered her sincerest apologies and explained that she was leaving before their arrival, as she had to get back to Miranda.

Sarah exited Spencer's dwelling and hastened her pace outside. He followed, grabbing her arm and turning her to face him. 'Sarah, my dear, I delayed professing my love for you and now that you are here, I'm certainly not going to let you go … Sarah, you can't just stand here and say you don't feel it too! We are connected, you and I. We are kindred spirits, soul mates! Our paths have crossed and reunited once again for a reason.

'Let's assassinate our dreaded hindrances, obstacles and constraints. Instead, let's adopt the wise old spirits of love, freedom, courage and basic laws of nature. Can't you see I'm in love with you – and you can't deny you're love for me still?' he pleaded.

'That's it!' Sarah murmured solemnly almost under her breath. Numb, she peered down avoiding eye contact.

'What are you saying, Sarah? I can't believe you're saying it's over, it's only the beginning.' His hands cupped Sarah's jawline, tilting upright towards him.

Sarah was silent for several seconds. 'Yes, Spencer, it is only the beginning! I want to burn it all!'

'Burn what exactly? I'm not following you.' Spencer creased his forehead with a frown of perplexity.

'Burn the book!' Her heart sang with joy. 'Not in the literal sense of the word, Spencer. Destroy all misconceptions, perceptions and interpretations. You said the "wise old spirits", that's precisely it! As the "Epistles of Wisdom" hold many secrets and special sacred philosophies!' She tugged at her gold necklace. 'Look at this pendant Spencer, what do you see?'

His eyes heaved at that stomach wrenching moment, his heart launched out into a kind of ether and vacuum. 'A coloured star within a circular perimeter.'

'Exactly! You see, I have risen to a deep awareness, that we don't need books of sacred ideas or any religion to obey. Don't you see, Spencer? It's already ingrained in our souls! You know that will … that driving force? Some of us are conscious beings, yet we all have this energy to succeed. Do good unto man – that is the creed we have been searching for all this time. It's in all of us! Only if we rouse to the fact, we can be our own heaven and hell too. This negative entity engulfs our spirits adding to paranoia and fear, generating division.'

'It's up to us? Is that what you're saying, Sarah? The power is in you, right? Then stay with me! We can make *us* work. You've come to some deep awareness, it seems, and from your travels you've grown somehow, perhaps spiritually, what do the colours represent? Do they embody the system of the five great elements as in Hinduism? Earth, water, fire, air and ether – the space that other elements fill. Or perhaps as five wounds of Christ? Five senses, five points?'

'Oh my God Spencer! I love you so much. For arising hope and further speculation in me to delve deeper into the history of the Druze and its secrets. The five (or 'phive') pointed star must remain fixed, vertical, with the topmost triangle pointing towards the sky, for it is the seat of knowledge – and if the symbol is reversed, deception and wickedness will prevail.'

Sarah peered down at her Louis Vuitton multi-coloured watch. 'Yes Spencer, you are right and I have learnt, "Tourists accept, Travellers select". I just don't want to accept anymore! This isn't about you and me any longer, and that kills me more than you know. It's about the world, our universe … and we're all in a deep, deep sleep. Perhaps this time I may be a traveller.' Tears vied down Sarah's cheeks. Her eyes were like abandoned rocks submerged in chocolate millponds. 'I must get back to Miranda and Adel.'

Sarah stared up at the angel wing cloud waves in the sky and boarded her latest model mauve BMW wagon. She didn't even peer in her rear view mirror. She drove away from the one man who understood her heart and knew her soul. The one man who loved and admired her for the student and girl she was – and, now in her winged metamorphosis state, the woman and teacher she had become.

# Chapter Twenty-five

Sarah eyed the 'Book of Wisdom' that lay adjacent to the passenger's seat beside her. The love in her heart for Spencer felt like fiery spiralling darts through her chest, as she gasped amidst wild flowing tears. She wanted desperately to turn back and tell Spencer how much she loved him and that she wanted to be with him.

Sarah pictured when Jamal defined the *kamsa hadood* pendant of the coloured star and circle. Sarah clutched that very chain Jamal gave her around her neck and closed her eyes tightly.

She rotated her wheel in a westerly direction and stopped at the side of the road, leaving her engine running as she reached down and seized the spiritual text. She flicked through the pages and all she saw at that moment was ink on paper that resembled words. Sarah wasn't reading, but reasoning with life. That all religions are roads of the same divine source. She figured the reason she was here on earth was to figure something out, read the signs and put the puzzle together for the sake of humanity. Was she the chosen one? That was too big a challenge and too hard a burden to bear. Spencer had mentioned the elements and Sarah concluded that the first element is Ether: space or air, the essence of emptiness.

She felt she must hold a position, one of an alchemist, a traveller on a cosmic journey.

If reincarnation is true, a future onus is placed deep within an ancient memory. Sarah changed her frequency of thought. She didn't need to search for her kindred spirit any longer, as it rested right under her nose. Spencer was indeed the one and true love of her life, yet something inside her, summoned an inner awareness that the universe needed her more than she imagined.

Sarah rose above her pride, arrogance and judgment. 'It's not just me at all, damn it! We're all in this together.' She thumped her fist hard on the steering wheel. All of humanity and all the elements make up this communal work of creation – including all living organisms, plants, insects and animals. 'We are one': one nation, one race and one religion, hence the colours of the spiritual pentagram star portrayed in this Druze symbol merged as one.

Sarah recited as she held her chain and observed the pentagram star, thinking to herself that both Jamal and Nabila mentioned the pentagram has a special number hidden inside, a universal thumbprint of God called the Golden Ratio, the basic belief that geometry and mathematical ratios, harmonic proportion found in music and light.

Green: The mind/farmer/life.

Yellow: the word/sun/wheat; the mediator between the divine and the material.

Red: soul/heart/love of humanity.

Blue: sky/faith/will.

White: future effect/indwelling/air/purity. Indivisible. The omnipresent ether, the carrier of light.

The Druze amalgamated philosophies on mysticism, cosmology, Hinduism, Judaism, Christianity, Neoplatonism and Pythagoreanism. This system applied religious elements in unanimity with one another.

'Aha!' Sarah sparked an internal glowing lightbulb moment once again, forming the notion that all religions are sharing one another's writings, thus collective consciousness must indeed prevail. The spirit brought the five elements into natural synchronisation.

Sarah found her astonishing kindred spirit in 'ether' – an unseen substance that infuses the whole universe and connects it to each other.

The Divine Proportion – phi, music and sacred geometry – chanted repetitively in Sarah's conscious state. There her vision erased the restrictive ring, the gatekeeper perimeter that divided the colours and kept them from flowing out abundantly into the universe. 'Behold the free spirit paradigm shift.' The skies opened up in mystic fashion as she stepped out of her car cautiously and peered above. The glowing star presented itself once again, larger and more luminous than ever. Its warmth encompassed her being.

Beyond the rising sun in all its glory, she was already one and in sync with our universe. The kingdom of God. Sarah celebrated the mysticism deep within an evolved and enlightened soul.

> With you in my mind and dreams, I can cast aside the fears of my life now with you in it. High school crush, some would say, but it's much deeper and intense. Your deep blue eyes captured mine, at moments when time stood still.

> I'm not willing to brush this off as lust.

> Like two pieces of celestial dust – let us live and linger.

> Deep within ... deep within, the spark will never die. Heartfelt emotions running through me.

> I want to reach out and grasp hold of you, if only for a minute.

Deep within and within the deep I'm drowning at a deadly pace.

Oh Mr Fitz, out of all the high schools why did you have to waltz into mine?

Downing in sorrow.

Drowning in pity.

Drowning in visions of you.

So deep, deeper. Breathless. How can I escape these pent-up feelings? Throw a life buoy out to sea and save me from reality.

# Acknowledgements

First and foremost, to Blaise van Hecke from Busybird Publishing, for opening the door of opportunity with positive energy and grace. Blaise never questioned my writing abilities and made me feel like a writer.

My sincere appreciation goes to Kim Kearsey and Janet Reid, for their recommendations and giving me the light and hope to reach my goal.

Following my introduction to a young, talented and dedicated Beau Hillier, he not only edited my manuscript but also enhanced its substance by aiding its growth process, hence motivating me.

Thich Nhat Hanh, Simon Parkes, Steven Spielberg, Mel Gibson and Tyrese Gibson unknowingly sparked an inner desire to write from deep within my core.

I express my gratitude to my brilliant son, Sami Merhi, and gifted daughters Lana and Savannah. They are my 'love triangle' who inspired me to go on.

In addition: Nizar Ashkar – a man of depth and brilliance of mind, for taking the risk to put *Deep Within* out there into the Druze community – I'm thankful for his belief, faith and for being a trusted friend. Sonia Monia Daou, for shedding light and lending her hand of hope. I also cannot fully express my gratitude to an enlightening soul, Peter Davis, for expressing his belief in my novel through a 3CR radio podcast of chapter sixteen. My sincere appreciation goes to my dear friend Lyndon Stephens, for his encouragement and faith, reading my novel many times at its early teething stages.

For all  people not mentioned here, you are all elements  and entities that contributed in some way, shape or form to bringing the love circle to life – you indeed know who you are!

Finally, and certainly not last, my dear mentor Craig David Featherstone, for providing essential support, superb guidance and a kind listening ear for my constant passionate outpourings surrounding *Deep Within*.

# About the Author

Ms Fadya Alameddine was born in Melbourne, Victoria to Lebanese Druze parents who immigrated to Australia in 1971 before the civil war broke out in Lebanon.

After graduating college in 1993, she was accepted to a Double Degree of Arts at Deakin University, although she deferred to travel with her parents overseas.

In 1996 she started work in a doctor's surgery as a medical receptionist, and has owned and operated numerous cafés and small businesses. More recently Fadya has completed a Certificate 3 in Aged Care and her Diversional Therapy Certificate 4 at Holmsglen Campus in Chadston. She currently works at Andrew Kerr Aged Care in Mornington as a PCA and diversional therapist.

Mr. Nizar Hajj
President of Druze Community Charity of Victoria
info@druzevictoria.org.au
www.druzevictoria.org.au